A MILLION TOMORROWS

KRIS MIDDAUGH

Rebel
Publishing

Copyright notices

Today
Words and Music by Randy Sparks
Copyright © 1964 Primary Wave Songs
Copyright Renewed
All Rights Administered by BMG Rights Management (US) LLC
All Rights Reserved Used by Permission
Reprinted by Permission of Hal Leonard LLC

International use of "At the still point" from **Burnt Norton**, the first book of **The Four Quartets** by T.S. Eliot granted by Faber and Faber, Ltd, publishers.

US/Philippines use of "At the still point" from **Burnt Norton**, the first book of **The Four Quartets** by T.S. Eliot granted by HarperCollins Publishers, LLC, publishers.

Rebel Publishing
78 Buena Vista Ave.
Suisun City, CA 94585

This book is a work of fiction. Any references to historical events, real people, or real places are used fictitiously. Other names, characters, places, and events are products of the author's imagination and any resemblance to actual events or places or persons, living or dead, is entirely coincidental.

Copyright © 2024 by Kris Middaugh

All right reserved, including the right to reproduce this book or portions of this book in any and all forms whatsoever.

For information contact:
Rebel Publishing, Rights Dept., 78 Buena Vista Ave, Suisun City, CA, 94585.

Book cover design and layout by
KUHN Design Group | kuhndesigngroup.com

Library of Congress Control Number
ISBN 979-8-9898635-1-8

To Bill, whose dual dreams, one sleeping and one waking, first began then fulfilled this work.

CHAPTER ONE

As a reader, it may interest you to know why I—who have had so much time to do so—am choosing now to write my story. The fact is, I'm old and perhaps close to dying. Again.

Since deciding now was indeed the time to expose my truth, and looking back over my life, I've often thought about sixth grade. You may scoff, but sixth grade is pivotal in a young person's development. Balancing precariously on the edge of adolescence, as one does at that age, even the smallest situations and experiences and people can have monumental sway. That final year of elementary school, I was lucky enough to have a teacher named Miss Gibbs. She was young and, I thought, very beautiful. She was new to teaching and brimming with ideas and faith; in us and in all the possibilities secreted within our 11-year-old bodies. Even now, I hope I have lived up to her innocent and ardent belief in me.

During that sixth-grade year, Miss Gibbs often read aloud to us for a half-hour or so following afternoon recess. She introduced to our class everyone from Roald Dahl to Mark Twain with a skill and gusto that rivaled any acting on television. Accents were her specialty, and when she read *David Copperfield*, I was continually mesmerized.

I'd watch her mouth form the words that came out sounding like Victorian England—or so I imagined from my obviously limited knowledge of the time and place. Many in the class listened with their eyes closed, heads resting atop arms folded on desks. But I stayed wide awake and watched. As I did, everyone from the delightful Clara Peggotty to the evil Murdstone and criminal Uriah Heep came to life before my very eyes and through Miss Gibbs' intoxicating lips.

I've also thought frequently of the opening lines of that Dickens novel. They were short, precise, and factual: "Chapter One. I am born." Were it not so familiar (to lovers of Dickens at least) that it now borders on cliché—I might have begun this story the same way. Or in some adjacent variation. "Chapter One. I am born. Again." Or perhaps, "Chapter One. I am reborn."

But the more I thought about it, the more I considered the need to tell everything and how best my story should unfold. I realized that mine is a story not nearly as simple as "I am born." My life's tale has beginnings, to be sure, but it is perhaps a tale more about endings—or what we think of as endings—with, I hope, a little insight into both. Thus, my story both begins and ends with death, with death in the middle too. As you will see.

I begin this story on a Friday morning. That day, I was back in Lien's office. Dr. Lien Tran, psychiatrist. She, of the well-appointed office, buttery couch—both in color and softness—and solid wood coffee table with delicate and detailed corners that belied its sturdiness (much like Lien herself). Everywhere were simple and ornate reminders of her travels, her heritage, her love of art and beautiful things.

Lien was actually one of the first people I'd met when I began my residency at the UCSF Medical Center at Mission Bay in San Francisco. The location was my first choice for residency, not only (although I told others *mainly*) because it was part of the prestigious UC Medical system, through which I had completed medical school, but also because it was within easy walking distance of the ballpark. I knew my work hours would be long and busy, but they'd been long and busy for years at that point, and still, there was always time for baseball.

I ran into Lien—quite literally—late and frazzled on my first day at Mission Bay. I grew up in the Bay Area, in San Jose, to be exact, so I had no excuse for underestimating the number of people who would be on the ferry that morning. It was the height of tourist season, after all. Thus, despite my plan to arrive extra early, I couldn't get a seat on the boat I'd lazily assumed would have plenty of room and ended up tearing through the halls of the hospital, tardy and sweating, despite the typical cold of a July morning in San Francisco.

Unfortunately for Lien, she had not quite made it to her office when I plowed through, dinging her on the elbow and sending her into an almost comical twirl. Had she not been a seasoned rock climber—tiny but solid and balanced—she almost certainly would have ended up sliding, high-heeled lower half and well-manicured upper half, sprawled all akimbo across the checkerboard linoleum. As it was, my Nikes squeaked to a sudden halt, and I lurched before turning around to begin apologizing profusely and obnoxiously loudly as I tried to overcome my embarrassment and breathlessness. Lien was polite and gracious, as always. I was a mess.

"Oh my God, I'm so sorry! I just...I...are you okay?" I babbled.

"It's fine. I'm fine. But I think you're in the wrong building, Dr. Roberts."

My nametag. I understood instantly. This wasn't the first time someone had made the same mistake.

"No. I'm right, I think. Zamora?"

"Oh yes. Straight ahead. I'm sorry, I just thought..."

"The tag. Yeah, I know."

I was still breathing hard. Red in the face. She was serene. Smiling. Taking in the details of my plight with compassion and well-trained insight. She was then, as well as on that certain day, and always, the Lien I could count on.

"So... straight ahead?" I asked.

"Yes. To the end, then a right. You'd better be on your way, Dr. Roberts. And welcome aboard."

"It's Perry, and thanks!" I yelled over my shoulder, already back in my sprint and halfway down the corridor.

That Friday, the one on which my story truly begins, and the one that introduced me to death, my own and others, I was beyond residency — if barely — and in the middle of yet another session with Lien, Dr. Tran in this professional setting.

Do you know what it is to dangle off a ledge for so long that your arms become locked and your hands calloused in such a tight, incessant grip that it becomes...normal? Part of life? I'd been that way since medical school. My life was cliffside; every minute, a study in perilous equilibrium and committed resolution to not let go, to never begin a fall that might be endless. Lien was perhaps not the first, but ultimately the only person to not only see my tenuous position but to also insist I at least *try* to climb back onto solid ground.

I never knew my father. He died of throat cancer when I was a toddler. But for me, his cancer was an abstract — the word people said to me that somehow related to my fatherless existence. When my mother suddenly confronted the same beast midway through my first year of med school, it was very different. Cancer roared into our lives, baring teeth and breathing hot, rancid breath on my mother, myself, and our lives.

Despite a dire prognosis—stage four, ovarian—mom didn't give in easily. She seemingly tamed the wild for at first weeks, then months, then three full years beyond what any well-educated specialist believed possible. She had promised to—and almost did—see me walk at my graduation and match with my preferred hospital. But then, well, the "but then" was why I was in Lien's office again that day.

Our sessions were irregular as far as scheduled appointments, but she fit me in when I needed, or when *she* felt I needed. Actually, in the beginning, it had been quite a struggle for her to agree to see me at all. Lien was nothing if not ethical and proper. But I think she eventually understood I would see no one if not her. Faced with that trolley problem, she took a typically utilitarian approach—me being a physician and all—and opted to help the one in order to save the five.

And so, we were there that day. She urging me to detail my latest dream, nightmare in truth, and I, flustered, fumbling while trying to find a way to say the words without conjuring up the memory that had left me once again sweaty, heart pounding furiously, the night before.

"It's okay, Perry. Take your time."

It wasn't the time; it was the courage. I wasn't sure I could muster the reliving. But I closed my eyes and reassured myself I was safe in Lien's familiar office (as she had taught me to do in situations like these—and there were many of them). I inhaled deeply through my nose and exhaled through my mouth. Another gem from Dr. Tran's bag of tricks.

"I was back at the hospital," I began tentatively. "Everything was pale green and white. The doors were shut, and I didn't know where the sound was coming from, which door she was behind, but I could hear her calling my name."

"*Dr. Zamora. Dr. Ruben Zamora forty-one oh-six. Dr. Ruben Zamora, forty-one oh-six, please.*"

The perfectness of the intercom's abrupt intrusion almost made me laugh. But instead, I just stopped, thankful for the reprieve. I reminded myself to thank God or the Universe or whatever later.

"That's me. I'm on for Ruben this afternoon."

"Incredibly convenient."

I couldn't help but grin. "Isn't it though?"

"Later then? This evening?"

"Game tonight. Sorry. But I'll catch up with you Monday. We'll plan something."

Lien's highbacked swivel chair, the one that matched the couch so perfectly, was facing the door when she raised her voice to say, "We'd better!"

But I was already out the door and halfway down the hallway.

Ruben was Dr. Zamora. The selfsame man I'd been trying to find my first day at Mission Bay. He was the head of oncology and my mentor throughout my residency. I was covering for him that day. Not his regular appointments, but emergencies only, which justified the abrupt ending of my nightmare session. I told myself to remember to thank Ruben as well.

Our Cancer Center is a building separate from the main hospital in which Lien had her office. So, I once again found myself dashing through hospital corridors and bounding upstairs instead of fidgeting through a meandering elevator ride. There was no code called, but I wouldn't have been paged if it were not an urgent situation, so I ran. When I finally reached Zamora's station, I had to grab the wall to bring myself to a quick stop while I caught my breath.

"I'm taking (quick breath in and out) Dr. Zamora's (one more gulp of air) emergencies."

"Oh, Dr. Roberts. I knew that. I should have been paging *you*. What was I thinking?"

Doris Maynard.

She was older than Zamora by a decade and had been his nurse for three times that long. Others in the department were younger—much—and probably more on-the-ball, but you couldn't beat Doris for experience, wisdom, or kindness.

"No (catching my breath now). It's fine. I was just…in the main building…and…so what do we have?"

"Well, she's kind of a special case, and it is an emergency. Not life-threatening, but I knew Dr. Zamora would want to see her personally. Or as close to personally as possible."

She smiled, and I smiled because I liked Doris, and I also liked flattery.

"And what's going on?"

"She fell. Beverly. The patient, Beverly Bowen. In the parking lot, just a few minutes ago. She was on her way home after her infusion. Someone saw her go down and called for help. It's her arm and some scrapes. She's, umm, not happy."

People not happy went with the territory in oncology. On the other hand, there were countless examples of courage and strength, and laughter and love, even with the cavernous maw of death blocking every pathway to the future and every window to light. In this department, there was as much inspiration and joy as there was resignation and sorrow.

I would never begrudge any patient, including this woman, this Beverly, their righteous and rightful anger and pain. So, I braced myself for whatever she might need to let out. I could absorb whatever my patients needed to spew into the ether. I understood and felt I owed them at least that much. It was, I believed, part of their treatment. Thinking I was prepared, I opened the exam room door.

The way most of our exam rooms are designed—sink, counter, and supplies on the right as you enter, exam table and computer to the left—our patients, if seated on the exam table, have their back to us when we open the door. So it was in this instance. I entered as I often did, eyes half on notes, half navigating my way into the room. But this time, I stopped, hit with a wave of…something.

The smell was everywhere. It was soft, full, and flowery. Yet there was a cleanliness to it as well. Like home. Or a doorway between home and a wide-open field of…something. Lavender? I didn't know enough about flowers or gardens or the outside, really, to be able to make an accurate identification. But I breathed in deeply and tried.

"Oh. It's overpowering, I know."

This assured, amused, and not at all angry voice belonged to Beverly Bowen.

"I'm sorry," Beverly Bowen began. "My friend. Well, my friend and wannabe yoga instructor, Lily. She's very into essential oils and that whole friend-of-the-Earth, bohemian thing. She pretty much douses me in lavender and lemon every time I have a treatment."

I grinned slightly, like an idiot, I'm sure. But my words were caught somewhere I couldn't reach. I was slightly off balance, like in a movie when the camera recedes and the scene pulsates. Much later, Beverly would say, "Like *déjà vu*, right?" But it wasn't as far removed as that. It wasn't a feeling of having been here before. It was more a feeling of…here I am. Where I should be. Where I was always meant to be. Finally.

Beverly Bowen tried to make up for my awkward silence. "I know Ruben is out of town, but I thought they'd still send an oncologist."

I woke from whatever fog I was in and laughed a little. It was the same mistake Lien had made that first day. The same mistake people made over and over with a quick glimpse of my nametag.

"No. I'm an oncologist, alright," I said with what I'm sure sounded like an idiotic stumbling.

"See, here on the bottom? Oncology. GP is my name, not my specialty. Dr. GP Roberts."

"Ah, I see Dr. Roberts." She smiled now too, and it was like her whole face, eyes, nose, mouth, teeth, skin conspired to light the room, light me from the inside.

"And your friends, they call you GP?"

"No. No. I'm just Perry. They call me Perry."

I was stammering like a child, like my childhood self. It was reflexive when it came to explaining or even talking about my name. But this time, it was more than that. I was flustered.

"Well, I'm happy with Dr. Roberts at the moment…my arm and all."

Here I'd been lost in my own, what? Miasma? And she, Beverly Bowen, was in pain. I quickly resumed physician mode, took a cursory glance at the bruise and swelling, and knew instantly it was likely a broken wrist. I'd be ordering X-rays in a minute, but first, a short physical exam.

"Let me take a look here. I'll try not to cause you any pain…"

Beverly was in her sixties; Doris had said as much when she summed up the situation. She was about the age my mother would have been. Slightly older, actually. But somehow, I could see the truth of her behind those blue eyes bookmarked by laugh lines and set within a face that had known much time and laughter and pain, too.

Beverly Bowen's skin turned gooseflesh when I touched her arm, and I looked up to make sure she was alright.

"Does that hurt?"

"No. It just. I just…"

And there was a pause from both of us that involved a kind of synchronicity I had never experienced with another patient, or another human being for that matter. It was a moment that was only a breath or two and a small portfolio of heartbeats, but also familiar and forever. We caught our breaths and ourselves at the same time. She laughed a little. I quickly returned my gaze to her arm.

"It's fine. Well, of course, it's not, but no…no pain from your… touch," she said finally.

I ordered the X-rays then. The machine would come to her, so I tried to make Beverly comfortable and asked Doris into the room so she would know what was going on. I wanted to stay to be sure everything went as it should, but I had so many other obligations.

"Did someone drive you here?" I asked.

"No. No. On my own."

"Really? You understand that weakness and dizziness are, among other things, side effects of your chemo? It's important to keep yourself safe."

"Well, it's been fine up until today. I'll do better next time."

"You need to. You've got to be careful. So, maybe an Uber next time? Someone here can help get you to and from the car. Or have a friend come along. You know, just be aware of the changes going on in your body."

She bristled a bit.

"Oh, I'm aware," she said curtly.

I sounded patronizing. God, what an idiot.

"I'm sorry. I didn't mean to imply otherwise, of course. I just want to make sure you stay safe."

She laughed again slightly. A sad little kind of laugh.

I'd managed to double down on my own stupidity. Now, I wanted to be away from this room, this situation, and Beverly Bowen. All of it had become a portal to feelings I didn't want to have or remember.

"Well, I'm going to leave you in Doris' capable hands. I'm pretty sure you've got some kind of fracture there, so we'll figure it out exactly, and I'll have someone come in to cast it for you. I've got a lot to take care of before…"

"The ballgame?" Beverly Bowen asked.

The surprise surely showed on my face, and I flushed a little at her intuition. But she nodded at my Giants t-shirt and laughed.

"You're not going to miss a Friday night against the Dodgers, are you?"

"Never," I replied quickly and with probably a little too much force.

"Lifelong fan?"

"Who isn't?"

"Now, that's the correct answer for sure."

Here is something you should know. I am going to tell you things that you, as a reader, may think, at best, strange or silly and, at worst, a lie. But before I ever dared or challenged myself to leave this testimony, I went round and round with my own thoughts. What could I safely say? What would make anyone believe? How did I make myself seem credible and not, well, crazy? The decision I ultimately came to was that I needed to and must, with every word, with every comma and quote, be as truthful as I possibly could be, no matter the cynicism or the cost. I tell you this because in that moment and in a thousand other similar and cascading moments afterward, I knew. I just knew.

What I knew then was that I could sit with Beverly Bowen and talk baseball for hours. I knew that she would just *get* the obsession I'd shared with my mother, who had shared it with both my father, her husband, and my grandfather, her dad. I knew she would understand the nine-inning connection baseball gave me to both these men, whom I'd never known. Baseball, I instinctively understood, was a portal that was not only the opening to myself but to myself with Beverly. I knew, too, that she knew. We communicated in a world of others but also in a world that included only the two of us. Here is proof if you need it and if you want to believe my story or are willing to try to believe my tale.

I really did have other patients to see and much to do if I were to be able to make it to the game by its 7:10 start time. So, I tried to break out of this unsettling new place, get myself back to the real world of average people and typical problems. I wished Mrs. Bowen the best and told her I hoped to see her again sometime.

"It's not Mrs.," she corrected me. "It's Beverly. Or Ms. I suppose if you'd rather. But definitely not Mrs." She held up and twirled her left hand to show the evidence. "Never quite got around to it."

I smiled and was somehow glad about that. I started to leave again, smiling at both Beverly and Doris as I did so. But she stopped me.

"And what about you, Dr. Roberts? *Perry*. But that's your middle name, G.P. Roberts? Why not use your first?"

I paused to gauge her question. But it wasn't rude or even overly inquisitive. There was a grin. A twinkle. Seriously, that's the only way I can describe it: a twinkle in her eyes.

"Well, you know. Some first names are…better…better suited than others."

Now I was anxious to be gone and reached for the door, but Beverly, ahh, Beverly…

"You know," she said with feigned nonchalance, "when I was a kid, I had a favorite pitcher. A Giants superstar."

"That so?"

"Mmmhmm. Cy Young Award winner. All-star. Hall-of-Famer now."

"Lots of great Giants pitchers over the years."

"Oh, to be sure. But he was way before your time anyway. Lots of fans your age have probably never even heard of Gaylord Perry."

I flushed again and wanted to be gone before Doris noticed the red I felt rising in my face.

"You'd be surprised what some of us younger fans know," I said, and was gone.

I caught my breath a hundred or so feet away from that exam room and Beverly Bowen. What the hell was that? What had just happened?

CHAPTER TWO

I never got back to Lien that day or for a week or so after. So, I never got to discuss with her my latest dream…nightmare. I knew my "therapy" wouldn't be truly effective if I wasn't, as Lien put it, "forthcoming," but I'd already talked again and again about so many dreams and memories and speculations and tears. Too many tears.

Maybe it was because I was in therapy, trying to deal with…everything…that various parts of my many nightmares had begun to coalesce into a kind of Frankensteinian conglomeration of the worst parts of each. The dreams were never exactly the same, but they almost always contained some or all of the same haunting elements: There was that eerie green and white coloring; "ghost-hunter hospital lighting" is the way I'd first described it to Lien. The color tinted all the doors and hallways that extended and moved beyond my grasp with each of my slogging, slow-motion footsteps.

Faces. There were lots of creepy and oblivious faces, and me trying to yell for help, but no voice able to exit my mouth. Me trying to dial for help over and over again (though I was within a hospital, that same familiar hospital) yet somehow unable to hit the right numbers: 9—1—1. It should be so easy!

Then, my mother's voice. Exactly as it always sounded. So clear and so correct: asking for me at first, then calling for me. Then the heart monitor, louder and louder and louder—as if Edgar Allan Poe were writing the script for my dream. One more glance down the extending hallway. Then, white light growing so bright it's blinding. I'd shield my eyes, grasp and grapple for a door handle, any door handle. Then me crying and trying to scream and my mom pleading and yelling for me and me frantic, knowing that she was dying...again.

Sometimes I woke at that point. Other times, I'd hear the beeping turn to flatline. Still other times, my mother's calling turned to screams of pain or, worst of all, laughter. Like genuine, maniacal laughter.

Why? Why that laughter?

The first night—that first night I met Beverly Bowen—I thought about both her and my mother. I hadn't read Beverly's chart extensively—didn't know her entire history—but she was weak from chemo, her bones becoming more brittle from the same, and her balance obviously affected. She'd been battling this for a while. And Beverly Bowen was older than my mother was during her own fight. I'd thought about that combination of factors. I knew—so well—cancer's incessant, insidious agenda and the nettled path Beverly Bowen was being forced to trod.

For years, I'd craved but dreaded sleep. The nightmares from which I suffered were unpredictable but consistent, seemingly inescapable. Now, I feared Beverly Bowen could become mixed up in my ethereal green and ghostly white purgatory. And while I wouldn't have believed my sleep patterns could get worse...they did.

I must have slept. I mean, I was alive, so I must have been sleeping. I remember reading, well, being forced to read *The Bell Jar* in high school. In the book, Sylvia Plath's protagonist, Esther, complains again and again about not sleeping. At one point, Esther claims she hasn't slept for seven days. Seven days! Even as a teen with no medical training, I knew that couldn't have been the truth (as her mother tells Esther). But over the years and through unrelenting personal experience, I had come to understand that it was Esther's truth, just as it was now mine. During that time, the nights seemed endless, my sudden insomnia uncontrollable. But, at some point, I always fell into darkness. And when that reprieve came, it was short and deep. If I dreamt at all, I didn't remember. *Thank God.*

Exactly a week later, without having had the chance to spend another session with Lien, I was grabbing some lunch at a little sandwich spot I frequented when I had enough time or when I especially needed to see the sun — if there was sun. Samay was with me.

I'd known Samay for years. We'd been in med school together, and he'd started his residency — anesthesiology — a year before I began mine and, like me, stayed on at Mission Bay. Victoire had too, but she was a whole other story.

Samay was second-generation American. His dad, driven and accomplished, had emigrated from India to the US when Samay was a toddler. As the only son of an impressive man, Samay was expected to excel, and he managed, with what seemed like minimal effort, to always exceed expectations.

Beyond his medical license and successful practice, Samay was an accomplished violinist and bashful polyglot. Few knew of his fluency not only in English but also in Hindi, Spanish, French, Italian, and Russian. There may have been more. I suspected he enjoyed being able to casually eavesdrop on foreign conversations (of which there were many in San Francisco), but maybe I was too suspicious…or becoming a cynic. Although, really, Samay held a pretty tight corner on that market.

He was at the sandwich shop almost every day. I'm not sure how he managed his schedule, but somehow, long lunches were almost always a part of it.

"Game tonight?" Samay asked as we sat outside in the cool July air, slight breeze blowing off the bay. "I mean, with most people, it would be an easy assumption, given your shirt and all." He nodded toward another of my Giants jerseys. "But seeing as how your wardrobe seems to consist solely of Giants gear and jeans, it's hard to tell."

Samay didn't hate sports, but baseball wasn't really his thing. One would think his devotion to cricket might have provided a natural segue into America's pastime, but…not so much.

"Yep. You should come. Pediatric Cancer Awareness Night. No VIP ticket for you. But I'm sure there are still gameday seats."

"So you're going alone. Again." It was not a question. It was a statement laced with mock frustration.

"Well, my best friend won't come with me, so yeah."

"Dude. I have an actual date. You know, with an actual other person? You should try it sometime."

I laughed. After all, he wasn't wrong. But since Victoire and I had split nearly three years prior, I'd just kind of lived my life without trying to find someone else to bend and force into it. I was about to begin my usual "doth protest too much" schtick, but luckily, we were interrupted.

"Perry, Samay, not surprised to see you both here. Nice day for it."

It was Dr. Zamora, Ruben. Always welcome, but in this moment, especially so.

"Game later?" He too nodded at my jersey.

"You know it."

We asked him to join us, but he explained he was just getting some quick sun and picking up lunch. "No rest for the wicked," he said. Ruben turned to go but then hesitated as if a thought had suddenly found him and required his speaking. "You know Perry, Beverly Bowen will be in around three. Why don't you come down say 'hi' and take a look at her progress? She mentioned how well you took care of her the other day."

This caught me off guard, and I tried hard to feign nonchalance as if she hadn't been, as the song says, "gentle on my mind" since that Friday, two weeks before.

"Beverly…Oh, sure, I could do that. How's she doing?"

"Come and see for yourself," Ruben said over his shoulder as he walked away.

I turned back to Samay to find him smirking. "Duuuuuuude. Beverly, huh?"

"She's just a patient, Samay."

"Right. Right. So, your cheeks turn all Pikachu like that when you talk about any patient?"

Honestly, I had felt the heat rush to my face, but thought I was hiding it well. I told you Samay was smart. But I didn't understand anything that was happening connected to Beverly, and who knew if there was anything to understand anyway. Thus, I immediately went into denial mode.

"What? There's nothing…"

"Uh—huh."

"Seriously, Samay. She's old enough to be my mother, maybe my grandmother!"

That was a ridiculous exaggeration, and my protestations were too loud. I felt immediately like the Apostle Peter. I hadn't denied her three times, but why did it feel like such a betrayal?

"Okay. Calm down, dude. Whatever you say."

"I'm just…you know…it's just ludicrous."

And there it was. Three times.

CHAPTER THREE

Like a schoolboy, I'd been watching the clock all afternoon. At five minutes before three, I casually announced to my nurse that I was heading over to Ruben's office to check up on a patient.

"It's someone I saw the other day when I was covering for him. Not a big deal, so feel free to call me if you need me. I just thought I'd go over and see how the patient is doing. Dr. Zamora asked me to, actually. But really, go ahead and, you know, call if I'm needed."

I took a breath when I got into the stairwell to climb up to the fourth floor, and seriously, what was that? In general, I was a man of few words, saying what needed to be said and not much more—at least in a professional setting. I could see Adeline, my nurse, looking at me like I was a child overcompensating for a sensational lie, but I couldn't stop my mouth. This was getting ridiculous. But as I clunked deliberately up the dozen or so stairs, I told myself my unnatural behavior was due to stress, lack of sleep, and my caseload of patients, most of them like Beverly—some better, many worse.

"Ah, Dr. Roberts, you made it," Ruben said as I entered his office.

Ruben Zamora was a kind and formal man. I'd never seen him in anything but a suit and tie, and his tanned skin and greying hair made him something of a dashing figure. If you listened hard enough, you could hear the faint memory of an accent in his speech, which was otherwise velvety and precise. I caught the full measure of his eloquence when I heard him speaking Spanish, and I was jealous of the conversations he had with Samay and many others. I would like to have known him in both languages. In short, Dr. Zamora was everything anyone could hope for in a mentor and friend.

"I never want to miss a chance to learn from you," I said. "You know that."

"Well, you flatter me as always, but this is less about learning and more about connecting—which is actually the deepest form of learning, of course."

"Of course."

I said, "Of course," but it was instinct, and it wouldn't be until much later that I had the time—took the time—to parse through those words and truly understand them.

And then a deep breath through the door to Beverly Bowen, who sat once again on an exam room table but now looking much less bedraggled and much more in control—healthier even.

"Oh, Dr. Roberts. This is a pleasant surprise. Come to check your handiwork?"

"I thought Perry might want to see your excellent progress," Ruben explained, "and it is excellent progress."

The break had been clean and simple, a "green twig" break at the wrist. Her cast ended below the elbow, and she'd fashioned a sling out of a piece of material—a scarf maybe—that matched her meticulously lovely outfit. The colors in her clothing brought out the color in her face, her cheeks, and her blue eyes. I looked in those blue eyes again, and I swear, I saw that same damned twinkle.

"You look wonderful, Mrs. Bowen," I said, then instantly wondered if I'd chosen the wrong word, been too effusive. "But I didn't do much 'handiwork.'"

"Oh, but you did. You set me at ease that day, and I needed it badly. And wonderful might be a bit much, but I'm feeling pretty good now," she said, then laughed just a bit. "At any rate, this (she raised her broken wrist slightly) got me a reprieve from chemo, so I'm not mad about it. Plus, I got to meet a fellow Giants fan, so it all worked out rather well, I'd say."

"Infusions begin again in two weeks, agreed?" Ruben asked with what was actually a command and not a request.

"Yes, doctor. If you say so, doctor," Beverly said with mock seriousness. She then turned to look at me, address me directly, specifically. "Going to the game tonight?" she asked, moving her eyes to my jersey.

"Yes. Of course. My Friday night routine."

"Ah, got it. That's a very official looking shirt you've got on. Is there a name on the back of that jersey, perhaps?"

"Maybe…" We were joking around now. It was our own private joke.

"I think I can guess, but if you turn around and drop your lab coat, I could be sure."

So I did. Obedient. And happy to be so. It was there, of course, as she suspected.

"Thirty—six. Perry. Good man."

And I wasn't sure if she meant my namesake or me, but either was fine.

"Well, maybe I'll see you at the game tonight?" I asked.

"You just might, as a matter of fact. Where will you be?"

"First base side section two-ten. Not the closest seats in the house, but lots of good folks around me."

"Oh my, season ticket holder? You're serious, then. Bring your glove to every game?"

"Very serious. And one does not go to the ballpark without a glove. I'm not a savage. Though I'm also not quite a full-season ticket holder…yet. But I'll get there."

"I'm sure you will. Well, if I see you, I'll come say hi," she said and smiled, and my heart leapt. I wasn't sure why, but it did.

It took me about half an hour, maybe less, to walk to the ballpark from the hospital. Game time—for most night games—was 7:10, so it was generally no problem to get there on time if I planned things right. In fact, I was often early. Those pregame hours were when I had gotten to know some of my fellow 210ers. There were a couple of folks who truly had season tickets, but most of us were only aspiring toward that and, in the meantime, indulged in multi-packs: groups of tickets for weekends or promotions and giveaway dates or bundles of games against certain teams, like the loathsome Dodgers, or our friendly foes, the A's. I'd gotten to know most everyone who attended as many games as I did, and we'd built our own little ballpark community.

We checked in on each other's lives within the confines of Oracle Park but didn't see each other beyond stadium walls—well, except for an occasional foray to nearby Momo's or The Public House if a victory had been particularly sweet—again, this mostly involved the Dodgers.

It was a real feat to get out of the hospital on time that day. It felt like absolutely everyone was vying for my attention or suddenly had a need to talk to me about the most inane things. It seemed somehow conspiratorial. I just wanted to get to the game.

Finally, just when I thought I was free and making my escape on the Third Street side of the Center, something—my past as it were—caught up with me.

"Let me guess. Off to the game, I imagine?"

Victoire.

There she was. Looking as beautiful as ever despite being well into her pregnancy. Six months, maybe? Seven?

"Whoever said you didn't know me?" I asked.

"Wasn't me because I know every little thing about you, Dr. Gaylord Perry Roberts. I think I might even know who bought you that jersey you've got on there."

"Still my favorite present ever."

"Still looks good on you too."

Our relationship had always been—even at the beginning—more comfortable than passionate. I liked that about it. Victoire did too, until she didn't anymore. Until, I think, she got tired of me not moving beyond ease and comfort or, at least, beyond what was familiar. Proving that sometimes, what's familiar can become very uncomfortable. In one of the final scenes of our relationship, Victoire accused me of wearing my issues, that is, my all-consuming guilt and grief, like an old coat. She wasn't wrong. My coat was heavy and tattered, I knew, but such a part of me that I was unwilling to shed it, despite the sun and warmth—very much including her—around me.

We broke up. She moved on, married one of the medical center's administrators a year or so later, and now was expecting their first child. The weight of my coat became undeniable shortly after their wedding, and that's when I began seeing Lien professionally. Still, there was nothing truly acrimonious in our split. Just that realization that we were no longer in sync. We'd looked down one day to discover the tickets we each held were bound for different destinations.

She was happier now. I knew that.

"My mother tells me you haven't RSVPed for the baby shower. You'll be there, right? Samay's coming. You'll know everyone there. Grand-mère would love to see you again."

"Well, why didn't you tell me Grand-mère would be there? If that were on the invitation, I would have RSVPed instantly."

"Well, now you know. You're coming, right?"

I had somehow thought that if I waited long enough to respond, the whole thing would just sort of slide out from under my life. It wasn't that I didn't want to be there, celebrate with Vic and Michael, it was just…a lot. A reminder of where I was and where I could have been, maybe should have been. Still, she had that happiness glow, the one you really do see in so many pregnant women. I'd seen it again and again (though sadly, and in such cases quite obviously, not always) during my OB-GYN rotation. And now, with Vic right in front of me, practically blinding me with maternal light, how could I refuse?

"Of course. Of course I'll be there. Just *try* and keep me away. And tell Grand-mère I'm going to be pretty upset if there aren't some crabcakes and beignets on the menu."

"I tell her that, and she'll start cooking today just to be sure there's enough for next week."

"Now there is a perfect woman."

"As if you'd know a perfect woman if you saw one."

She was right, of course. I had a problem with not being able to see what was right in front of me. But maybe my hyperopia was actually helpful—just not for myself. It seemed like a lot of our conversations ended with one or the other of us saying something we both knew to be true, something sad and irreversible.

"*The rivers, they flow only one way, n'est pas?*" Grand-mère would say.

I promised to respond formally to the RSVP so Victoire's mother would have an accurate headcount, then we said our goodbyes in earnest, and as I hurried off down Third Street toward the stadium, I kept turning over that phrase in my head, "perfect woman, perfect woman." But perfect applied to a human being didn't mean infallible or absolute. Rather, it seemed to me to mean perfectly fitted. So both members of a "perfect couple" stabilized each other like mortar, filling in small personal gaps to form something, if not perfect, at least whole. And an image of a smiling woman with a broken wrist drifted through my mind.

If I'd gotten to the ballpark when I hoped, I would have been able—with my Pediatric Cancer Awareness Day VIP ticket—to walk on the field to "Triples Alley," where there was complimentary food and beverages, including all the beer I could drink. But, though I did arrive ahead of start-time, all the free stuff was already packed up and put away. Happily, I still got my Buster Posey beanie, which was guaranteed with my ticket. It was all for a good cause, so I couldn't be mad, of course, but I was hungry and thirsty and frustrated for not planning better. Though one could never plan on Victoire.

I grabbed a crab sandwich and a beer—forty bucks I didn't plan on spending—before heading to the 210, where I plopped into my familiar seat just in time to catch the pregame activities. A young boy and girl, each no more than 7 or 8 and both obviously battling cancer, took turns throwing out the 'first pitch' to thunderous applause and, I think, some tears before dignitaries gathered on the field to present something to someone.

"Giants fans, please welcome to the field former Giants catcher Buster Posey and a very special guest with a very special gift for the BP28 Foundation and its fight against pediatric cancer."

A smattering of applause, and I looked down just in time to see several children holding an oversized check while a woman in a Giants jersey and a broken right wrist took the microphone.

"Thank you everyone. And thank you, Buster and Kristen Posey, for your tireless work on behalf of pediatric cancer patients and pediatric cancer research. On behalf of the Daniel E. Bowen Charitable Trust, I'd like to present this check for fifty-thousand dollars that we hope will allow you to further your admirable work and aid even more amazing children like Tamara, Emory, Aubrey, and Jackson, who are here tonight as a testament to your good works and to help me present this check."

Much more applause and kind and gracious words from both Buster and his wife, Kristen. I'm sure they were wonderful words, though I heard none of them. Instead, I was sifting through shock, rattling my head, and feeling like an idiot for not having had a very obvious two-plus-two add up to four prior to that moment.

That Beverly Bowen, as in the Bowen Cancer Center and new Bowen Cancer Research Lab and a half-dozen other Bowen-related places and things in and around the city. What an idiot I'd been! No wonder Ruben wanted me to follow through with a patient I'd barely treated. We were always courting dollars and the people who had the most of them. Much of our work and certainly our research depended on them. I tried to quickly go through everything I'd said during our two brief encounters, but it was all a blur. Good lord, I hoped I hadn't embarrassed myself or, more importantly, my department or the medical center as a whole. Thank all that is holy, I was two sections above the field and out of sight—hopefully out of mind too—of Beverly Bowen. *The* Beverly Bowen.

"You look like you've seen a ghost, son."

This was Mr. Bob Antonelli. He and his wife, Sheila (but always Mr. and Mrs. Antonelli to us 210ers), had held their season-ticket seats since the park opened. Diehard fans since before Oracle Park, they'd had upper-deck season tickets at Candlestick. Third base side. He said he much preferred the first base view (as did I) and remarked often how much warmer Oracle was compared to The Stick. It was a rare day when it wasn't cold enough to warrant a jacket or jacket *and* blanket at Oracle, so I couldn't even imagine how cold it must have gotten at Candlestick Park. But everyone in San Francisco agreed we'd take the cool over the heat and humidity at someplace like Truist Park in Atlanta or Nationals Park in D.C.

"Do I?" I asked while trying to gather myself.

I was embarrassed, not for baring my emotions before the Antonellis, but for being so foolish as to not recognize one of my workplace's greatest benefactors. And even for not understanding her devotion to the cause of cancer research, which had been going on for decades, long before her own ironic battle began.

"It's just…I…well, I've met Beverly Bowen, and I didn't realize she'd be here tonight…well, I knew it, just didn't know about the check and all."

"Seems like a nice lady. Donating all that money. Fifty—k! She must be loaded!"

"Yes. I guess so. She must be."

Then I felt like a fool all over again. A fool on repeat. Story of my life.

Everyone loves a good back-and-forth game. Lots of excitement when your team takes the lead, then has to catch up again and again. But I'll take a nice blowout any day. By the seventh inning stretch, we were up by six even though the Rockies were having a great season, far better than our own. I tried never to leave a game before the last pitch, whether we were down by a dozen or up by the same. But, already, the stadium was beginning to thin out, and the Antonellis, along with Tom and Jenny Peterson and Ricky Castro, were gathering up stuff in preparation for an early exit. The Antonellis were in their 70s, so it made sense, but I didn't really blame anyone for heading home or to a local bar an inning or two early. I was taking the last ferry back across the bays — San Francisco and San Pablo — to Mare Island, where I rented a little house that used to be a part of military housing for the former naval base there, so I was in no hurry.

Most of us were just sitting down after the traditional singing of *Take Me Out To The Ballgame* when the Antonellis began gathering their stuff, and an usher tapped me on the shoulder.

"Excuse me. Are you Dr. Roberts?"

Naturally, my first thought was a patient emergency. And maybe it was? Yes, I acknowledged I was he.

"Mrs. Bowen would like you to join her in her suite if possible."

Like a sitcom audience, my friends around me gave out a simultaneous, 'Eww — woo.'

"Perry's movin' on up!" Ricky yelled.

"To a de — luxe apartment in the sky — hi — hi," Andre Mills sang in his best baritone. That guy was always singing.

"Alright, alright, everyone. Calm down. She's a patient. Just a patient."

"Rich patient!" someone said. Patty Dearing, I think.

"Okay. Enough."

I looked at the usher who said, "Right this way," and I heard someone — maybe Patty again — yell, "We'll expect a full report tomorrow!"

Seriously, would the embarrassments of the evening never stop?

CHAPTER FOUR

'd never been inside a VIP booth. Never really expected to either. My mother kept telling me we were going to celebrate my med-school graduation by renting out a luxury box, and she was going to have "Congratulations Dr. Roberts!" plastered across the Jumbotron. Mom didn't quite make it to my graduation, though—honestly, I almost didn't either—but the whole idea seemed pointless and nearly cruel when Victoire mentioned following through with Mom's idea.

The usher led me inside an amazingly large box where maybe a dozen or so people milled about. They were all talking, laughing, drinking, eating—definitely not watching the game—though, given the score, I didn't judge them too harshly.

Beverly was seated near the windowed wall that looked out onto the field. Still first base side, but brilliant in its privilege. Outside the glass were three rows of maybe ten seats each. These, too, were off limits to the common riffraff in the stands. They belonged exclusively to the owners (or renters) of the box. Given her casual hand-off of 50k, I suspected this box was not a rental.

"Dr. Roberts!" Beverly exclaimed almost immediately as I entered her Shangri la. "I'm so glad you came up. Oh, but you were welcome to bring anyone with you. Wife or girlfriend or date…significant other…I mean anyone."

Now, she was the one running on and on with a blush creeping into her cheeks. Was she fishing for information? Didn't seem likely a woman such as Beverly Bowen would have to fish for anything. I'm sure she had people to do that sort of menial labor for her. I laughed. Smiled.

"Well, I'm not married, and it's just me tonight. And in general, no girlfriend…or boyfriend…no extraneous friends at all," now it was my turn. "I mean, all my Section two-ten friends would have gladly come up, but that might have been a lot. And a little rowdy for this set."

Now she laughed.

"Oh, you'd be surprised how rowdy this…, uh, set, can get. Bank presidents and booze, you know? At any rate, your section would have been completely welcome."

"I may hold you to that next time you're up here, and we're all, well…down there."

"I insist you do!" she said, smiling. And I believed she was really serious.

"Listen, Mrs. Bowen…Ms. Bowen…"

"Beverly or Bev or Bebe."

"Bebe?"

"My father's pet name. But I think you could use it. I think I might like you using it."

I paused to take this in. It was a funny thing to say, maybe. Especially given our very short previous encounters. Yet at the same time, it seemed natural and felt right."

"Bebe. Yes. I like that."

"And I do like you saying it."

"What I wanted to say…Bebe…well, what I wanted to do was apologize for not realizing who you were. I should have recognized the name. I'm sorry if I came across as…"

"As what? Caring and professional? Because that's how you came across to me."

"Did I? Well, then I'm glad. I mean, that's how I always want to come across to my patients."

I was stammering a little and feeling incredibly awkward. It was unnerving. Beverly—Bebe—was unnerving. I could have (and would later) easily find her birthdate on the internet, but I was sure she was at least sixty. Maybe older? That would make her roughly twice my age. And it wasn't that she didn't look her age—although she clearly had that hint of having been told of her own beauty many times—it was just that she wore it so well. She fit her years and lit them with something ethereal that lived within; would always live within. Of this, I was quite sure.

"And, of course, there's the fact that you carry the name of one of my all-time favorite players. Besides Will, of course."

I was so shocked to see her on the field, and again now, in this setting, that the jersey she was wearing barely registered. Twenty-two; Will Clark. Who didn't love Will the Thrill? I congratulated her on the choice of jersey, and we launched into a lengthy discussion of Giants' baseball history and the history of her life. Seems she was the only daughter, only *child*, of one of the earliest "tech geniuses" in the Bay Area. Daniel Bowen had begun working in early computing and military defense while in the Navy and right after college. She'd grown up on Mare Island! And had lots of fond memories of her time there. Of course, she and her parents lived in one of the big houses closer to the old hospital while I was renting an aging and boxy enlisted man's quarters that, incidentally, I loved.

Her dad had worshiped the Giants even when they were in New York, and their moving to San Francisco was something like heavenly proof the Bay Area was the right place to make their permanent home. Eventually, when her father retired from the military and began to build his empire, they moved to the Berkeley hills, still within easy access to Candlestick Park, where Beverly — Bebe — said they spent nearly every weekend and some weeknights as well. Her father made it a special point to include her in his love for the game, especially after her mother passed away (not from cancer, but perhaps even more tragically, in a boating accident) when Bebe was ten.

As the game wound down, and after Beverly introduced me to several people who seemed comic book caricatures of the words "captains of industry," we huddled together in two outside stadium seats and talked through the wind about what it meant to lose a mother. Apparently, the experience was much the same for a fifth-grader as it was for a fourth-year med student.

The Giants won handily – seven-zip. That was the good news. The bad news was the recording of Tony Bennett singing *I Left My Heart in San Francisco* that began wafting through the ballpark and the seagulls swarming the stands meant the end of the game, which also meant the end of our conversation and the end of being near Beverly.

I would have suggested going out for a drink or something, anything, but I could see the exhaustion settling in on every part of her and knew she needed to be home, in bed, resting…hopefully recovering.

I said as much after everyone else had left the box and only her driver (she had a driver!) was left standing dutifully at the doorway. I scolded her a bit about the foolishness of driving herself to treatments when she had a driver at her disposal. Bebe was appropriately admonished and promised to "take the car" next time. She would have to anyway, Bebe laughingly told me, because her little convertible was a stick shift, and well…she held up her broken arm again. Bebe also told me she had a nurse on call but insisted she would be fine on her own for the evening. Brave, I said, but perhaps a bit capricious.

She laughed at my word choice and told me I sounded like her father. Not the first time my generational standing had been questioned, and I told her that too.

"I think you need a nickname," she teased.

"Oh, yeah? Super Doc or something of the like?"

"Something of the like…" she mocked in a fake Perry Roberts voice. "Hmmm. You talk like a baby boomer—you certainly dress like a retiree…"

I feigned shock and insult.

"Boomer it is!" she declared.

"Like Esiason, I'm assuming," I said.

"Oh my God, listen to yourself. You know who Boomer Esiason is! How old are you again?"

"A very young and hip thirty."

"Hip? Seriously? Is that a word all the cool kids use?"

She found the whole idea hilarious, and good lord, how I loved seeing her laugh.

Beverly offered me a ride home—it was an easy detour on the way to her house in Berkeley (Not her childhood home, the family had long since progressed beyond that 3,000-square-foot shack.), but for some reason, that seemed too intimate, an acknowledgement of something that wasn't ready to be acknowledged. So I told her I liked riding the ferry and already had my ticket. She said she understood, and I swear when she said it, there was something of relief in her voice.

The entire night had been…intense…and I was happy to settle into the hour-long boat ride with a few dozen other fans. I looked around and could see they were all caught up in a kind of drunken exuberance over the win. But I was reeling, not only because of the game, but also because of Beverly, the bay, the San Francisco night air, the lingering sweetness of Tony Bennett's voice, and the perfectness of it all.

CHAPTER FIVE

We hadn't exchanged numbers, Beverly and I, or anything of the sort. We'd talked of the things closest to our hearts and shared mutual laughter that most others wouldn't have understood, but the act of sealing the deal with an entrance into our daily routines seemed somehow too risky, an admission of something neither of us had even begun to process, let alone accept.

Still, she was on my mind, and though I didn't bring those thoughts to light, in the shadows, I began counting the days since I'd seen her, since that night at the ballpark. It was my luck, I suppose, that I had access to the infusion center's schedule, and though it was natural for me to make sure my patients were taken care of—monitoring their treatments and checking nurses' notes—I began also looking for Beverly's name.

Her accident had temporarily halted Bebe's chemotherapy, but I knew it would begin again shortly. I wouldn't think of violating her privacy—overstepping, as it were—but just casually going through the schedule and happening upon her name well, that was just a coincidence. Nothing more.

When I finally did see an infusion slated for Beverly Bowen about a week or so later, I gasped slightly, and my heart beat noticeably faster. Ridiculous, I told myself. I rationalized the relief and anticipation as simple doctorly concern. It was good, after all, that she was once more receiving treatment.

I postponed—yet again—another session with Lien, brushing aside her multiple suggestions to schedule an appointment with a wave of my hand and an excuse about how busy I was. Samay was not as easily dissuaded. He was constantly peppering me with questions about the dating life he imagined for me. He had vowed never to settle down. Never to live a life of rhythmic predictability that he felt his very traditional parents led.

"Play the field, never yield," he'd told me at least a thousand times over the years. I always laughed and sometimes nodded my head to suggest an affirmation, but never saw his parents' obvious devotion and comfortable companionship as a negative. I was never sure what Samay was looking for. I'm not sure he knew either. I didn't have an example of parental *pas de deux* to emulate or even observe. But, the snippets of domestic life I glimpsed in the Shankar home and Shankar marriage—despite Samay's rolled-eye explanation that it had been arranged—seemed structured on mutual respect, curated comfort, and, yes, actual love.

Meanwhile, Samay's life seemed to me chaotic and hungry. He didn't know what he wanted; he just knew he wanted. And whatever it was he wanted, he wanted it for me too. But I was ever reluctant.

"C'mon man," he begged me a few days after the ballgame, "how long can a baby shower last? Even if we miss like the first hour, that concert is going to be going on way into the night."

I was trying to be sensible—thinking about common courtesy as well as the fact that I had zero desire to spend hours shoulder to shoulder with fifty thousand screaming, intoxicated, heavy metal fans. Don't get me wrong, I liked some of the bands scheduled to play at the all-day festival Samay wanted us to attend, but that kind of live experience after a toned-down afternoon of family celebration seemed not only incongruous, but frankly exhausting. Samay often chided me about my reclusiveness, telling me we were "only thirty, bruh!" but I felt the weight of those years, and they pressed on me in a way that sometimes made it hard to breathe. I felt forever burdened by malevolent forces working beyond my control.

Naturally, the concert was about more than music. Samay knew some girls who would be there; more than a couple for each of us, he said. That, however, didn't sway me in the way Samay hoped. All of it just felt like a lot of work…in the sun…with a pounding, rock and roll soundtrack. I knew I sounded like an old man, but quite honestly, I often felt like one. Life could be a lot.

"I was thinking Vic's parents and yours and my…me…well, I mean all of us could maybe have dinner or something after. You know, like old times?" I asked tentatively.

"Dude, we're not in college anymore. We don't have to spend time with our parents to make sure we get our allowance. We're free, man!"

I told Samay, maybe. "Let's just wing it day-of," I said. Which appeased him but was, in reality, just a delay I hoped would give me time to develop a plausible excuse not to go. It also allowed me to back quickly out of the conversation that, for some reason, had my head spinning.

Is that what our recurring "dinners with the parents" had been to him? An unavoidable and awful means to an end? When my mom was healthy, and even after she first got sick, I loved those times we went out as a big, jovial group. Victoire's parents—Martine and

Bernard Royer—sometimes including Grand-mère too, along with Samay's mom and dad—Hema and Kabir (but always Mr. and Mrs. Shankar to us)—and, of course, my mother, the winsome, inimitable, and effervescent Charlotte Roberts—Charlie to everyone who knew and loved her…and there were so many.

I'd never thought of these dinners as duty or obligation. To me, they were the first, and only, manifestation of an extended family that I'd never had. My mother, the only child of an only child, had few living family members, and all were quite distant in both relation and geography. She'd instilled in me that the two of us were perfect by ourselves. But in truth, it may only have been something we each said hoping it became truth for the other. Holidays were fine and happy, but to me, they felt narrow. The inclusion of the Shankars and the Royers and sometimes others of their easily accessible relatives felt like a widening: the expansion of a lasso that roped in exponential fun and joy and love.

How odd to think that those memories, so pleasant and precious to me, meant something entirely different to my best friend. I doubt Victoire felt the same as Samay, but then again, how well did I really know Victoire anymore? Or maybe ever? Still, I hoped Saturday would bring me back to what I considered the best of times and that Samay and Victoire—despite whatever their qualms might be—would be swept up in a wave of nostalgia and conviviality, and if not, I at least hoped they would humor me and my tenacious grief.

Meanwhile, Beverly's infusion was scheduled for the Friday before Victoire's baby shower. Normally, I would have been anxious to begin the weekend—and a Friday game—as early as possible, but I knew Beverly—Bebe—would be at her 1:30 appointment for three or four hours, which meant I had exactly that much time to casually wander through the infusion center and come upon her…quite by accident. The truth of the matter was that I normally spent very little time in the center. That was handled by our fabulous team of nurses, whereas I saw patients and strategized treatments three floors above. Of course, it wasn't completely unheard of for me to be in the area, but generally, if I were in the infusion center, I would have a very good reason to be there. Then again, on that day—although I didn't put words to the feeling—I had a very good reason as well.

I watched the clock all day, and by post-lunchtime, it was getting ridiculous. I felt the slowing of time as the clocks on my wrist and computer and office wall slogged through the minutes and teased me with sleepy movement.

Time often felt slippery and loose to me. It regularly held me captive in a way that cheated and manipulated my life. When my mother was ill and going through her own rounds of chemotherapy, time slowed and tortured us both. Later, time teased us—Mom most especially, most painfully—with hopeful promises that got cruelly broken as her cancer changed course, then sped up with a viciousness that hurled us both toward oblivion and loss. That last month was windswept and wild, collapsing everything, including time itself, around us. Then there was that day. That last day.

It was the very end of my OB-GYN rotation. Victoire and I were in it together, she loving every minute—having decided early on to make it her specialty—and me, anxious to move on to something I deemed more important, more urgent. I was focused on cancer eradication—or, at the very least, treatment and care. So there we were on the precipice of medical careers that would see one of us gleefully ushering in life and the other desperately clawing to delay the inevitable.

Throughout medical school, I'd made it a careful point not to let anyone know what was going on in my personal life. If I vigilantly curated who did and did not know about Mom, it made me feel like I had some kind of control over the clearly uncontrollable. Victoire knew, of course, and she often begged me—especially when I was looking particularly bedraggled—to tell my supervisors and school officials. But I would have none of it. It was a uniquely egotistic form of pride and self-flagellation that, as Shakespeare had put it (as if he knew my 20-something self), was full of sound and fury and signified nothing.

When I got the call, I was standing in a small gaggle of other students, discussing one of the patients we would be assessing that day. I'd been restless all morning and couldn't keep a medical thought in my head. My phone was set to silent, but when it vibrated in my lab coat pocket, everyone was aware. Dr. Hildebrand looked at me with an angry raised eyebrow and asked if there was something more important I needed to attend to. I said no, but Victoire shot me a look that snapped me into line, and I said, "Wait. Yes, there is. I'm sorry."

I didn't wait to hear her response; I just bolted out of the room and answered my phone breathlessly as I ran. I knew. Before Carmelita said a word, I knew.

"I think you should come, Mr. Perry."

Carmelita was from the Philippines. She was in her 50s, small and round, and a great nurse, fantastically caring. I'd told her a million times it was just Perry, but she insisted on the Mr. for me and Mrs. for my mother.

"It's her breathing. It's changed."

"I'm on my way!" I yelled into the phone as I ran through the parking lot.

My mother had chosen to spend her last days at home.

"I never want to see the inside of a hospital again," she'd told me when we filled out her DNR. I promised she would never have to. But racing down 101 trying to make the hour-long trip from the city to San Jose, I hated myself for ever agreeing to let her forgo any kind of care that might have kept her with me for another month or week or day or at least as many minutes as I needed to get through the damned freeway traffic.

"Her breathing. It's changed…"

Carmelita's words looped around in my brain as I sped down the freeway. I knew exactly what she was talking about. Already in my fledgling medical career, I'd seen it again and again. In slang terms, it was called the "death rattle." But in my experience, it wasn't a rattle at all. It was a giving up, a deliberate settling into the routine of not breathing after a lifetime of drawing breath regularly day after day, without giving the process so much as a thought.

People reaching this stage would gasp then sink down into a quiet, non-breathing only to gasp again when the habit of inhaling seemed nearly forgotten. It was a bit of torture for families, knowing the end was coming and hoping in some ways that it would simply come, yet dreading the longer and longer intervals between gasps. Each ragged gulp of air seemed a momentary triumph of will that yet claimed, "I am alive."

"Please," I pleaded, first in my head, then over and over again out loud, "please, please, please, please, please…"

I slammed on the brakes after screeching sideways into my mother's driveway. I bolted up the pathway to the front door only to see Carmelita open it and stand apologetically, tearfully. Time slipped again and tossed me from lightning bolt to treacle, and I struggled to lift my leaden legs up the stairs. I didn't shout "No!" and lay hands to cheeks in some Munchian way. Instead, I couldn't say anything. And I couldn't stop the tears.

After a forever of moments, I made my way inside and fell to her side. She was close-eyed and dreamily translucent in the hospital bed that took up the better part of the living room. As always, it was turned so she could look out the front window. I took her hand and cried into her soft, thin skin. Supplicant. Even in those first moments, begging for her forgiveness.

Now, here I was again, invested somehow in another woman with cancer and waiting for my cue to meander in as if I were casually assessing the damage being done to my patients that day on behalf of their quest for a cure.

Actually and happily, we had many successes. Even in the handful of years since my mother's death, we had become more targeted in our approach with better diagnostic skills and personal vigilance from a generally well-informed public. Money, as always, was a major prohibition against reaching everyone who needed help, but I had faith — and it took a lot of it — that someday, that too would change.

I knew that I had two patients whose infusion appointments roughly overlapped with Beverly's, and they were key to my plan. Obviously, I rationalized to myself as best I could, it was good practice to look in on Debby Linderman and Herbert Cross. It would be nice for them to see that their doctor was aware and around. I, of course, hoped and, in fact, expected them to know this, but going the extra mile (as I honestly always tried to do) couldn't hurt. But even as I told myself these things, I knew the truth of my heart, and I knew I was perpetrating this elaborate ruse for no one but myself, and for a reason I couldn't quite put my finger on. Not yet, anyway.

I waited until two before I took a deep breath and informed

anyone and everyone in the office that I'd be in the infusion clinic if I were needed. Nods and polite smiles met my declaration as clearly no one thought it odd or took special notice. Still, I cleared my throat and adjusted my lab coat as if I needed to reaffirm my title. Doctor. That's *Dr.* Perry Roberts, a person who definitely belonged in the infusion clinic.

It takes some time to get set up for the long process of receiving chemotherapy and other associated drugs. Vitals must be taken. We need to ensure pre-session medications have been ingested and have had enough time to begin working. And it's not as if our nurses pull a "bag-o'-chemo" off the shelf. Again, everything is highly individualized, and the process of making sure the right drugs go to the right patient is a methodical one. Then, there is delivering medicine to patients, most often via a port temporarily embedded just under the skin. Only then do the long hours of waiting begin; often three or more hours of drip, drip, drip.

Our clinic had televisions at each reclining patient chair, but many chose to read, or sleep, or knit or visit with a friend. In fact, Herb Cross (appointment time 11 a.m.) actually *was* asleep, and I ended up spending only five minutes or so with Debby Lindeman since both her daughters were by her side and involved in deep discussions about the wedding of one of them—Caitie, I think. Or maybe Cathy.

When I backed out of that visit as gracefully as I could (given I was completely intruding), I thought I might just leave. Why hadn't I considered that Beverly might not be alone? Or might not want me there at all? I turned to head to the closest of the two clinic exits when I heard my name in the form of a question.

"Dr. Roberts? Perry?"

It was Beverly, of course, and I turned with a smile that was relief mixed with the embarrassment of having been caught, unmasked, just when I'd decided to remain a phantom.

"Beverly!"

A little too loud. A little too much surprise in my voice. But neither she nor the woman seated beside her seemed to notice. I couldn't say something like, "What are you doing here?" But I also felt like I needed to say something, so, of course, I said too much.

"Well, I didn't expect to run into you today. I've got a couple of patients I wanted to check up on. Herbert Cross, he's in his eighties, and I like to make sure he even gets here and is tolerating things well, and then there's, uh, Debby Lindeman, although she's got her daughters here planning a wedding, so I didn't spend much time there either, and I was just about to head back up to my office and…"

I took a deep breath and made a real effort to shut myself up and regain something—anything—like a professional demeanor. "Well, how are you doing anyway?"

"I'm quite well, actually. And, as you can see, I took your suggestion and decided to bring someone with me this time."

"Oh, that's very good. I'm glad. Much safer."

"Yes, it is. Especially since I can't drive right now, remember?" She lifted her cast as she had the night of the ballgame and smiled…again. "Lily is much more fun than Ben, my driver—you saw Ben the other night—anyway. So…here we are."

"I'm glad," I said.

My smile lingered for what I thought might have been a bit too long, so I clarified. "I mean, I'm not glad you have to have this treatment, but I'm glad you have someone here with you and that you're being careful."

Now, we both smiled. After a second or two or fifty—I couldn't be sure—Beverly's companion cleared her throat and broke whatever was keeping Bebe and I somehow tied together.

"Oh, I'm sorry," Bebe apologized. "Dr. Perry Roberts, this is my yoga teacher, general health guru, and best friend, Lily Phanes. Lily, Dr. Roberts."

Lily smiled and offered her hand.

"Oh, I've heard all about you!" she teased.

If Lily truly were Bebe's yoga teacher, she looked every inch the part. Blond and lanky, she was dressed as if she'd spent the morning at Woodstock and had a tarot reading to do later that day. She was all health and youth. She couldn't have been much older than me, and perhaps younger—and fun. You could see the joy streaming across her face like sunlight. I liked her immediately. I couldn't imagine anyone who wouldn't.

Beverly quickly tried to mitigate both Lily's words and enthusiasm. She was embarrassed, it was obvious, and I relished finally having the shoe on the other foot.

"She just means…well, I was telling Lily how well the check presentation went and that I'd run into you at the ballpark, and well…"

Lily sighed before she spoke with the voice of a dreamy, 1950s teenager. "You talked for hours, apparently. As if you'd known each other your whole lives, so I hear."

"Thank you for clarifying, Lily. I'm sure Dr. Roberts has better things to do than chat with the two of us…"

"Do you, doctor? Do you have better things to do than talk with me and Beverly Bowen? *The* Beverly Bowen? Business mogul? Writer of songs and poetry? Baseball aficionado? Giver of donations? Sailor? Art collector? Worst yoga student ever?"

"Well, actually, I'd love to hear more about what exactly you've heard about me. Do go on…" I smiled at Lily and looked to see Beverly blushing like a schoolgirl.

"Alright, you two are hilarious. You can stop now," Beverly interjected. "And can we just go back a moment to that remark about my yoga skills? I mean…*one* of your worst I could see. But *worst ever?* C'mon, Lily."

"I stand by my words. But I still love you, Bebe, you know that. And I also know I need to stretch my legs. Maybe get something to drink. Anybody want anything?"

"Pick up a muzzle while you're out, will you?" Beverly quipped.

"Never. I'm an arbiter of truth and must allow it always to pass through these lips."

Lily sent Beverly an air kiss, winked at me, and cantered her way out of the clinic.

Now we sat in silence. In that moment, Beverly was everything I would come to think of as quintessentially her. Quiet and calm but open to everything and everyone around her. Always willing to shift the day's plans to accommodate another or rise to meet the whims of chance. Unflappable. Self-possessed. Peaceful in her own happiness. She was dressed in what I came to think of as classic Bev-style too.

Today in simple jeans but with a t-shirt neatly tucked and some kind of silky blouse thrown over the top. Blues met with a burst of florals that continued to the wide headband that hid the fact that her blond hair — troubled by the chemo — was mostly whisps now. Looking at what seemed to me like something of a glow that surrounded her head, face, and being, I realized that it wasn't so much that she didn't look her age but rather that she defied it. There was nothing about her that pointed to this decade or that. Nothing that said I belong with this group of retirees or that group of students. She seemed to exist outside the lines of normally well-drawn life-categories.

I was staring, as she was well aware, but she didn't shy from it.

"Well, Dr. Roberts, we meet again."

"I really wish you'd stop stalking me," I joked. And she didn't skip a beat.

"What a shocking accusation!" she mocked. "I assure you; I don't stalk. I actually have people who do my stalking for me. Lois is on my payroll, you know." She nodded toward one of the tiniest old women I'd ever seen. Dressed in a bathrobe and sleeping blissfully while curled up on her recliner receiving her infusion.

"I thought I recognized her," I countered. "Skulking around my gym this morning and the bar last night."

"You were at the bar last night? I'm shocked again! And on a work night? Unbelievable."

"I was on my way home, I swear. I just ducked in to try and escape the probing eyes of your spy. But Lois is tenacious."

"That she is…" Beverly's eyes drifted back to Lois and lingered. She knew and cared for this woman, I was sure.

"It's never fair," I said.

"No. That's the one thing I absolutely understand about cancer."

You would think that kind of talk and the sudden shift of mood would have pushed me to politely exit. But no. In fact, with every intimacy we shared, there came a desire that bordered on need to share more.

I asked about Lily and how they knew each other. She told a funny story of literally crashing into her in a health food store when Bev had first received her diagnosis and had vowed never again to let an impure, non-natural morsel of food or ounce of drink pass through her lips.

I looked down at the Coke can on the table next to her. She laughed and told me the effort had lasted less than a week, but the friendship she struck with Lily—who continued to live the lifestyle—had endured for close to seven years now.

"Seven years?" I asked in horror.

"It went away for a while. A nice long remission. Made a surprise reappearance two years ago and somehow regrouped and picked up speed about six months ago."

But she said that sentence in passing, moving quickly back to Lily and her yoga studio and her husband, Lucian, who apparently I would definitely hit it off with since he was a doctor too. She asked me about my work, my friends, my hobbies besides baseball, and what I did with myself outside of office hours. I didn't have much to say on any of those counts. Since Victoire and I had split, and since Mom, I mostly worked and followed the Giants, tried to avoid Samay's fix-ups and party plans, and generally kept my nose to the grindstone.

She told me about her father's death soon after she finished college. Taking over the "family business" (that was actually something of an empire) because that is what her father had wanted and, in fact, prepared her for. It meant giving up her own dreams—poetry and music—but she still tried to make time for those when she could. Though it was never enough time, she said. Never enough.

I mentioned that I'd had my own artistic dreams, painting and pen and ink, but they seemed frivolous and self-indulgent after my mom got sick. She asked if I'd martyred myself on the altar of cancer, and I said, in all seriousness, I didn't think so, but it did lighten my grief and maybe my guilt too.

With that, I began to try to gently coax the conversation back to her illness. What had happened? What was she dealing with? What—though I wasn't sure I wanted to know—was her prognosis?

I asked about the stress of becoming CEO of a Fortune 500 company as a post-grad twenty-something. She laughed and said her father had taught her how important it was to always surround yourself with the best people. She said the men—almost exclusively men in the beginning—who surrounded her father truly were the best and had helped her in ways too extensive and numerable to say. Her greatest regret—and she didn't think much about it being a regret until seven or so years ago—was taking up smoking when she also took up the mantle of responsibility for Bowen Global Systems. Her father had been a smoker, and she associated it with wisdom and power and… her dad. Plus, she said, it helped with her stress.

Bev told me she'd been "smoke-free" for almost a decade. Her quitting came more than three years before her initial diagnosis. Three years before, she'd had a section of her left lung removed and gone through her first rounds of chemo and radiation. When she'd received the news—two years prior—that the cancer was back, more extensive and more aggressive than before, she thought she might forgo treatment at all—it had been that bad the first time—but friends and coworkers had convinced her to try…just try. Unfortunately, she'd procrastinated—reluctant to confirm what she already knew was causing her coughing and fatigue and the lump on her neck. Now, she said, she was just buying time to put things in order.

I sat for a moment with those words. Beverly and the world before me became watery, and I wasn't sure if it was because I felt myself falling into some distant and boggy place or if it were as simple as my eyes welling up under the unexpected weight of her words.

I'd felt this before, not only with my own mother and the ending of things with Victoire but on numerous smaller occasions, infractions foisted upon my life like sharp, rapier cuts wielded by an unknown but powerful—perhaps omniscient—swordsman.

I didn't think my life was unique, and in fact, I knew that my circumstances, my decades of experiences, were far less traumatic and brutal than those of many others. But at 30, I figured I knew a thing or two about life, and what I understood it to be was a child's board game controlled by an arbitrary toss of the dice. And just when you thought those three moves forward were getting you somewhere, you could toss snake eyes and land on a space that might change everything—set you back—ruin it all.

What I thought I most understood about this game was that although we played parallel with others—often influenced by their choices, demands, and mistakes—ultimately, we were on our own. It was a solo journey, lost and won, over and over again, by that toss of the dice and the whims of the swordsman.

After several seconds—or maybe minutes, I couldn't be sure—I swallowed hard and said, "But treatments have improved radically. Surely there's hope."

Her eyes softened, and she tilted her head. Squinted, assessing me, the situation, and the future.

"Maybe," she said.

I tried to steer the conversation back to something innocuous, something day-to-day that would make everything normal again. I could see the corner of an open satchel by her side and asked her what she was reading.

"I'm not sure," she said and laughed at my puzzled expression. "Well, this." She pulled out the book. "Is an old friend. My favorite."

It was a dogeared copy of *The Great Gatsby*. Now I smiled.

"That's actually my favorite book of all time," I told her.

And then there was this, one of those moments I came to think of as links…our links. It was something like *déjà vu* but involved both of us, and I knew we both felt it. We'd talk a lot about it later, but I'll tell you more about that as we go along.

For now, what I need you to consider, to become invested in as you read this, is an understanding of the ways we communicated with each other. Because I can describe the scene and write out the remembered dialog, but I need you to take that extra step as a reader and try to feel what I — what we — were feeling and believe in those feelings. I've danced around the truth of my life with many people, family and friends, colleagues, and vaguely interested parties. And what I've come to know is that these kinds of linking experiences are far more common than we acknowledge. We've all felt them at one time or another. We might laugh them off or mock them. Maybe we find them eerie instead of life-affirming. But now, after so much has happened in my very long life, I believe with all my heart that such moments are gifted to us so we feel less isolated, that the game is not lost, and that indeed, we are *not* playing alone.

I hadn't come to any of these realizations in that moment. But a flood of connection washed over me and ran through my body. It animated our conversation as she quoted some of her favorite Gatsby lines ("There is no confusion like the confusion of a simple mind." And, "Reserving judgements is an act of infinite hope.") and laughed. She said she thought she could quote the whole book. I told her I thought I could, too, but didn't tell her the one line that came into my mind just then. It was actually a reversal of a quote, but it fit. Fitzgerald had said, "He looked at her the way all women hoped to be looked at by a man." But watching Bev laugh at herself and ourselves, then seeing her turn serious and philosophical over the meanings of books and relationships and life in general and having her eyes return to me again and again—the inside-out Gatsby phrase took hold in my brain and maybe my heart too. "She looked at him the way all men hope to be looked at by a woman."

Lily returned about a half-hour into our discussion about Gatsby and her other books. Instead of returning to F. Scott, Beverly, by that point, had decided to tackle Circe—something she said she'd been meaning to do for years.

I got up to leave—I had others who needed me after all, not to mention a game to get to—and wished Beverly well with the rest of her day and the rest of the treatment. Then, as I walked away, I silently willed myself to become the wizard of South San Francisco, able to alchemistically transform the timid and worldly medicine dripping through Bebe's IV into an enchanted, liquid, miracle.

CHAPTER SIX

Back in the olden days, dear reader, which is to say, when I was a child, twenty-five or so years prior, baby showers were completely feminine affairs. The prospective mother and her female friends and relatives would gather to offer presents, eat cake, and do other things to which men were not privy.

I'm not sure when these baby-celebration events changed, but at some point, they began to include everyone and their Aunt Martha, as my mother would say. Or everyone and their Uncle Harry, as might be more appropriate in this case. I didn't at all think that we humans, as a species, should regress back to gender-separated parties. Not at all. In fact, it seemed right to invite everyone to a kickoff to the game of life. And heaven knows any brand-new soul entering our dubious world needs all the love and support it can get.

But, as the only son of an only daughter, I had little experience with babies and was completely ignorant when it came to knowing what to buy, do, wear, or say on such an occasion. Luckily, and as if anticipating the general lack of baby-savvy among their friends, Victoire and Michael had registered with a local baby boutique as well as a ubiquitous department store. The boutique had fewer items from which to choose — a good thing for me since I found shopping in general to often be an overwhelming experience. So, I spent a half-hour or so in front of my computer looking to find the thing I thought Victoire hoped most to receive. I didn't mind spending when it came to Victoire, so chose the pricey cream- and rose-colored crib ensemble. I was about to click "buy" when I suddenly had the thought — strange though it was — of actually going down to the boutique to buy my present in person. I reasoned that I could make sure of the quality and also pick out wrapping paper and ensure the entire package wasn't damaged in shipping.

It was an out-of-character moment for me, to be sure. I shopped almost exclusively online, doing my best to avoid, at all costs, actually venturing into a store. But when a tiny bell tinkled as I entered Bella's Baby Boutique, I wondered why I'd shunned this experience for so long. I was greeted by an older, smiling, white-haired woman and the smells of linen and polished wood. A quiet calm enveloped me. *Why was a baby store so quiet?* But the reverence was palpable. The clothing, bedding, furniture, and accessories all spoke of welcoming something sweet and fresh and loving and loved.

After that day and throughout my long life, I shopped in many such stores at many times as I bought things for family and friends and, eventually, of course, my own children. But with each entrance into each shop, I remembered that first time, and that day, and the shower, and everything that came with it…like a promise. And everything that followed…like a gift.

The table of presents was already nearly overflowing when I arrived at the Royer's home in Foster City. Both Martine and Bernard — Victoire's mother and father — greeted me with sincere and hearty hugs and a chorus of "it's-been-too-longs." They were warm and loving people and had always made me feel like a welcomed addition to the family. Grand-mére was seated by the gift table, alert and beaming. She was well into her nineties at that point but as sharp and effusive as ever. She recognized me immediately.

"*Pierre! Bonjou pitit mwen!*"

She was tiny and wheelchair-bound and feisty and the closest thing to a grandmother I had ever known. She spoke English perfectly, with a slight and charming accent, but fell into Haitian Creole easily and languidly. I loved to hear her speak it but knew only a phrase or two myself.

She told me I looked well. That she missed me. She then pointed to Victoire and told me I needed to see all that I had given up and was missing out on. Yes, I agreed. I had surely made a mistake.

Ah, but no, she now changed her mind. It was good that Victoire was with Michael. They were *te fè youn pou lòt*: made for each other. I hugged her and told her I thought so too, and I was happy that Victoire was happy. All true things. She wanted to know all about my life, but what was there to tell? Not much had changed since the last time I'd seen her at Victoire's wedding. This made her scowl.

Then she wagged a tiny finger and told me, "*Ti Mari p ap monte, Ti Mari p ap desann.*"

I knew this expression. She'd scolded me (and many others) with it before. According to Victoire, the literal translation was, "Little Marie will not go up. Little Marie will not come down." In other words, nothing's going to change if you don't do something.

"Touché, Grand-mére. Touché," I said with a smile. Though this time, for some reason, the little singsong saying fell heavy across my heart.

The afternoon progressed like that. Seeing people I hadn't seen since my life included Victoire and a whole host of associated pleasures and pains. There was so much food, I knew Martine would be sending portions home in plastic containers to guests lucky enough to fall in her favor. I wandered around the living room, patio, poolside and had almost decided to make an early exit when I was found…again.

"Bruhhhhh-thuhhhh!"

It was Samay, on the other side of the pool, waving me down, beer in hand, an unknown girl at his side. He mouthed the words "stay right there" and they made their way toward me.

"Holy hell, dude, I've been looking for you everywhere! Can you believe this spread and that pile of food inside? It's better than when we used to visit on weekends!"

He wasn't wrong. In our poor and cloistered college days, a weekend spent in Foster City meant clean sheets, lounging by the pool, and copious amounts of creole delicacies courtesy of Martine and Grand-mére.

"I know, right?" I agreed. "Just like old times…well, except for Victoire being married to someone else…"

"And about to have a baby any minute, dude. Don't forget that."

I hadn't. Not for a second. But I smiled at Samay's cleverness, the way a parent indulgently smiles at a child telling an age-old and familiar joke. Amid a kaleidoscope of churning and overlapping feelings, I could still put on my "everything is fine" face and support my friend in front of his date. Girlfriend? Friend? Cousin? Escort? Who knew with Samay.

It was a running joke when we were in college and sadly, but perhaps not unexpectedly, it continued to this day. Who would Samay bring to this party or that dinner? How would he ditch her after his three-date max? Samay's biggest fear in life was boredom, and somehow, he'd come to believe *comfortable* and *content* were synonyms for boredom. If that were true, how I longed to be bored.

Samay introduced me to the girl at his side (And I do mean girl. Twenty maybe?).

"This is my friend Matilda," Samay offered.

Her first words to me as I shook her hand?

"That's Matilda. With a 'Y.' M-A-T-Y-L-D-A."

As if I would interject the 'y' into any other spot in her name. As if I'd be writing her name out any time soon…or ever. She had two dates to go, max.

"Nice to meet you, Matilda with a 'y,'" I said while I shot a look at Samay, who shrugged his shoulders and smiled.

I had absolutely nothing to offer in the way of conversation with this girl, but didn't want to appear overtly rude by talking over her about a lifetime of shared experiences with Samay. So, it was a relief to hear Vic calling us from the doorway to the house.

"Perry! Samay! Ma - ty -yl -da! Could you come here for a sec?" She drew out Matylda's name to four syllables in what I was sure was an act of mockery, but Matilda-with-a-y just smiled. Oblivious.

Inside, Victoire took us into her confidence. In a whispered tone as we huddled in one corner of the kitchen, she said it was time to cut the cake, but she was uncomfortable with opening the presents afterward.

"There are so many!" she said. "Who knew there would be so many? It's embarrassing!"

"An embarrassment of riches?"

I knew the voice, but it was incongruous with the setting. I teetered a bit, reeling from the unexpected juxtaposition of two disparate parts of my life crashing into each other with a violent insistence.

It was Beverly Bowen. She emerged from behind Michael, who had just joined our secretive group.

"Oh, Bebe! You're right! But you'll know what to do! Tell me what I should do!"

"Don't open them," Bev said decisively.

It was the same advice I would have given. Of course, my reasoning would have been based on the solid foundation of time, and Bev's was based on the nebulous notion of feeling.

"Honestly, some people are able to give more than others. You don't want to make anyone feel less-than because they couldn't spend as much as someone else. Every gift is priceless in its own way. Don't ruin that for anyone."

"You're right, as always, Bebe. That's exactly how I feel. See, Michael?"

Michael's look was surprised. Surely Vic had been arguing to herself alone, with her husband never offering any advice on the matter. But Michael took the undeserved blame with kindness, understanding, and obvious love. More obvious than I had ever been and perhaps more than I was capable of.

"Just make an announcement—together—before you cut the cake," Beverly instructed. "Thank everyone in advance. Tell them all how much you love and appreciate them and maybe say something about wanting to spend time with each of them instead of making them watch you open gifts…you know, something like that anyway."

Victoire looked to Michael for support in this, her hour of etiquette-need.

"Sure, I'll do the talking," Michael said. Again, the better man than I. "C'mon, let's get that cake cut. It looks too delicious to let it just sit there."

And off they went to the living room and the decorations and everyone and everything that said love and baby and new life. Samay and Matylda tagged along behind, and I was left alone with Beverly.

"Hello again, Dr. Roberts," she said, leaning toward me conspiratorially. "Fancy meeting you here."

Bebe looked healthy and happy and quite beautiful in a long, flowy dress in purples and pinks. She wore a kind of headwrap thing that matched the outfit and somehow enhanced her face in a way that even the most well-appointed hairstyle never could.

"I didn't know you knew Victoire," I said slowly, carefully. Still wading, as I was, through this new estuary of my life. "…And Michael, too, of course."

"Well, for better or worse—in this case definitely better—when you donate a lot of money to a hospital, you get to know a lot of people who run said hospital. Michael and I met a half-dozen years ago when I decided to fund the research center. He was pretty new to the administration game then. He's come a long way. They both have."

"So, you know, then? About Victoire? About Victoire and me?"

The look on her face made it obvious she had no idea what I was talking about, and she stammered out a confused, "You…and Victoire?"

A blunder. A massive 'faux pas' if I were trying to mimic Grandmére. It wasn't that I was trying to hide it in general or keep it secret from Beverly in particular, but an admission of that sort inevitably involved walking backward into a past I didn't really want to visit again—or talk about, or explain—especially now.

Still, I'd opened the door, and there was nothing to do but walk through before it could be closed and locked tight once again. And, in truth, the entire afternoon had already been a long pie-fight of sequestered memories being tossed in my face again and again like so much merengue and whipped cream.

"We dated in college and med school…well, we were involved for quite a while, actually," I explained slowly, carefully. "It was a long time ago."

"Was it? Could it have been? How old are you again? Twenty-five?"

"I'm thirty!" I announced a little too loudly, and I knew I sounded like an idiot.

Beverly laughed at that and looked at me. She'd been teasing me, I could see now. She leaned in and I could smell a delicate perfume that might have been no more than soap, but that fell on me like a cloud of Beverly. As Bebe began to speak, she drew even closer and I could feel her warm breath on my ear.

"I like Michael a lot," she said, then fell into a whisper, "But I think Victoire may have missed the boat."

And I felt the entirety of the scene and her delicate words run through me like a warm, liquid confession.

"It might have been me who missed out," I responded quietly, and with my eyes closed. She was so close; I couldn't allow myself to see, only feel.

But after a moment, the sounds of the baby shower and the world grew louder around me. I could hear Michael making his gift speech, and I opened my eyes, drew in my breath, and backed up quickly.

"I mean, it was my fault. I…changed. I couldn't…I didn't want…"

Beverly looked at me softly, without judgement, but with a furrowed brow.

"It's okay," she finally said, "I've been there."

And as she smiled, I felt I knew everything about Beverly Bowen but also nothing at all.

Samay came back into the kitchen to ask if we wanted cake, then stopped short. I could see him gauging the situation.

"So…you two know each other?"

I took the lead before Bebe had a chance. "Oh, sorry. Yeah. Samay, this is Beverly Bowen. We met when she broke her arm a couple of weeks ago, and I was on call for Ruben…"

His eyebrows now raised in recognition while he continued to puzzle out what he'd walked in on. As he did, 'Y' Matylda and Samay's parents drifted in looking for him. We were surrounded.

"Everyone, this is Beverly Bowen," I began re-introductions. "Beverly, this is my friend Samay and his friend Matylda…"

She started to interrupt, but I was already there.

"With a 'y,' I said with great emphasis. "And these are Samay's parents, Kabir and Hema Shankar."

Beverly now raised her eyebrows and seemed suddenly very interested.

"Oh!" she said. "Any relation?"

Samay didn't seem surprised, but I was perplexed, and Matylda was completely clueless, which, to be honest, seemed to be her continual state.

Kabir laughed a big hearty laugh—he was a big, hearty man—and assured her, "No. No. It's a very common name in India. But I will let you in on a little secret: I have at times told certain persons that he is my cousin!"

He seemed delighted with his lie, and Bev and Hema laughed now too. I smiled but must have looked as ignorant as I actually was. Bebe turned to me.

"Don't worry…way before your time," she assured me like a teacher forgiving a new student on the first day of class. How could I, a generation removed, possibly understand? She touched my arm benevolently, smiled again, and said, "Google the name when you get a chance."

Then she and the Shankars were chatting away, and Samay, Matylda, and I shuffled off to claim our cake and sit at the kids' table. Not really that last part. It just felt that way. I was a little hurt, a little angry, and more than a little bit humiliated for some reason. After the cake, I absolutely could not resist skulking off to a corner to type 'Shankar' into my phone.

Top hit. Right there. Apparently, everyone in the Google universe but me would have known to ask, 'any relation?' when introduced to the Shankars.

Per Wikipedia: *Ravi Shankar, KBE, LH was an Indian sitarist and composer. A sitar virtuoso, he became the world's best-known expert on North Indian classical music in the second half of the 20th century and influenced many musicians in India and throughout the world.*

At first, I read it as "satirist," and I didn't get the connection between comedy and classical music. But then I re-read and was educated.

"I knew you'd do it." It was Beverly behind me. I nearly jumped out of my skin, and my heart beat wildly. "It's a good trait, you know, to be willing to learn. Ever heard a sitar?"

Oh! Now things started to make sense.

"Heard? Or heard *of*?" I didn't try to hide my generational gaffe.

What was the point? Everything around and including us, was true and obvious and incurable, both literally and figuratively. What did we have, if not honesty?

She laughed and said she actually had an album — vinyl — of his.

"You ought to come hear it sometime."

"Are you inviting me to your home?" I asked in a way that was a joke, but of course, not. If I'd taken a moment, I might have been more cautious. But, in something like a reflex, the words were out before I had time to stop them.

We looked at each other, and she cocked her head as she had the day of her infusion. Sizing me up once again.

"Maybe," she drawled. "I'm…" she started to say, then stopped, tucked an imaginary lock of hair behind her ear, force of habit I assumed, and began again. "I'm actually about to head to Lily's for a very casual dinner. We do this a lot. She worries about me eating… would you like to come?"

I had to catch myself from blurting out an immediate "Yes!" But somehow managed to retain a tiny bit of composure.

"Lily won't mind if you just show up with an extra mouth to feed?"

"Oh, you don't know, Lily! She won't mind at all. Especially if it's you."

"Me?"

She flushed and dipped her head before looking me in the eyes. "I just mean she liked you, you know? She'll be happy to see you again."

"I'll be happy to see her again too," I said. Again, with honesty.

"Oh good! My driver's outside. I'll call Lily from the car and let her know."

I said the quickest round of goodbyes I possibly could. Told Vic I'd see her Monday and met Bebe at the door. She stepped out first, and as I closed the door behind us, I caught a glimpse of Samay looking our way.

CHAPTER SEVEN

Berkeley proper is the capitalistic reality of much of the Bay Area. Here, property is mostly small and eclectic and also incredibly expensive. In the hills above the town, as in Oakland and San Francisco, loom the mansions of the monied elite, but below, amid the subdivided or renovated Victorians and various-styled cottages and even modern makeovers, there remains the illusion of middle-class mobility. Though, in truth, the price of these homes — even the smallest — teeter in, around, and well over the million-dollar range.

"We're almost there," Bev said as we turned onto a beautiful, mature street that featured home after stately home.

Take away the cars, and it might have seemed completely normal to be clomping down the boulevard in a horse and carriage. It was as if we'd entered a portal to another era.

"Démodé," Beverly said under her breath.

I looked at her with a soundless question. I didn't know the word, but I knew somehow, she was voicing what I was feeling. She continued to search the neighborhood as we drove slowly, almost silently.

"Should I look it up?" I asked.

She suddenly came back to me and chuckled. "No need," she said. "It's just a word…"

"That means?" I pushed.

"Oh, you know, old…antiquated," she answered with a dreamy kind of detachment. "Kind of like me…"

This was the first—though not the last—time I heard her say anything slightly self-deprecating or outright negative about herself, especially about her age. It stung.

"You're not old," I countered, perhaps too fiercely. "And you're definitely not antiquated."

It seemed like a long time before she returned from her reverie back to the present and answered, "Hmph. Maybe…maybe…"

We pulled into a short driveway. Lily's house was a true painted lady. A skinny, garishly colored (greens, burnt orange, yellows) three-story Victorian. I couldn't quite imagine how a yoga teacher and health-food guru could afford such a place, but then I remembered Bev had said Lily's husband was a doctor of some kind, so it at least made a little bit of sense. Although, as I'd soon find out, this was but one more thing about which I was completely mistaken.

Beverly told Ben, her driver, to go ahead home, we'd call when we needed him, or we could always call a ride-share service or something.

He was, however, concerned and insistent. "You call me whenever you need me, Ms. Bowen. It doesn't matter how late."

Beverly touched his arm and told him he was sweet and how much she appreciated him. By then, Lily's husband, Lucian, was standing in the front doorway, wine bottle and corkscrew in hand.

"Welcome, welcome Beverly and Beverly's friend!"

Lucian seemed friendly and gregarious—much like Lily herself. As we got to the doorway, I could see he was about my height (which is to say, 6 feet or thereabouts) but stockier and with darker hair than my brown. I judged he was a handful of years older than me from the few streaks of gray at his temples.

The interior of the Phanes' house was as bohemian as I would have expected from Lily. More brightly and thoroughly colored than the exterior, the large and open main floor was an explosion of vibrant hues, cushiony furniture, eclectic tchotchkes, plants, and pillows… lots of pillows.

Beverly and I were led to a vintage, tufted, blue couch, and wine was poured. Lily yelled greetings from the kitchen, and dinner smelled delicious.

"So, Perry," Lucian began, "Lily tells me you're a doctor. Oncology, is it?"

It was always strange to crash into the fact other people had been talking about you — maybe discussing you at length. It was especially unsettling when they were people you barely knew or didn't know at all.

At that point, I was a man who kept much to himself. And I mean that in both the physical and mental sense. I had few close friends and tended to avoid talking about myself, my life, and my circumstances with even them. Being so tight-lipped had definitely contributed to the breakdown of my relationship with Victoire and even affected my therapy with Lien. In fact, about six months into our sessions, Lien had needed to sternly admonish me (in her soft, psychiatrist voice) that we would not accomplish much if I were not "more forthcoming."

I had made great strides within the insulated walls of Lien's office but not much outside in the real world. Yet, here, with Bebe, Lucian, and Lily, amidst the color and comfort and wine, I didn't mind. I wanted to be a part of something. This something. This someone.

I told Lucian that yes, I was an oncologist, but not Beverley's, and then recounted our meeting, though I was sure he knew the tale. He asked how I had come to choose the profession, and I even talked a bit about my mother and her battle, briefly though—the kind of overview you can give without tears.

"Perry is an artist at heart," Bebe ventured.

"That so?" Lily asked as she entered with a tray of cheese and veggies.

I started to deny it, but Bev answered for me. "Oh, it's true. He's a painter. Of course, I haven't seen any of his work yet, but word on the street is that it's quite good."

"The street?" I asked. "Really? The street?"

"Oh yes, yes," Bev went on with her fanciful story. "People are talking about it everywhere."

"Very bored people," I said. "Who know nothing about art."

But even as I spoke, it warmed me to think that Bev had remembered this detail I'd shared that night at the ballpark. It felt like it wasn't so much a detail as it was elemental to the deepest part of me.

"Oh, you have to show us some time, Perry!" Lily said. "That way, we can get to know the real you. The true Perry."

I smiled and blushed, I'm sure. The truth was, I'd carried a sketchbook around with me for most of my life. I'd drawn comics and caricatures for my high school newspaper and often wandered around the Bay Area looking, sometimes for natural spots and sometimes for people to sketch and later paint. I looked now at Beverly in this vibrant, animated setting and wished I had it with me. Wished I could sketch the moment and keep it framed and with me forever. But I'd given up every part of my artistic life when my mother became ill, and now it seemed an inaccessible fragment of what used to be when I was far younger and far more naive.

I appreciated Beverly's blind trust in my talent, but I was uneasy talking about — even thinking about — my long-lost artistic dreams and quickly steered the conversation back to a comfortable place.

"So, Beverly tells me you're also a physician, Lucian?" I asked.

"Oh no, not a physician."

"I said doctor," Lily clarified. "And he is."

Lucian was modest and indulgent toward Lily. "Neuroscience," he explained. "I'm a cognitive neuroscientist. Ph.D. A doctor without the prescription pad…unfortunately."

"Oh, that's fascinating," I told him, and I was quite serious. "What kinds of things are you working on? And where?"

Lucian explained his relationship to UCSF and said he spent a small portion of his time at Mission Bay, though at the main hospital and not the cancer center, obviously. I was quite engrossed and willing to listen much longer, but I heard a kitchen timer go off and Lily announced, "Dinner's ready!" so we all exited to the dining table for a feast of vegetarian lasagna, French bread, and a salad with more ingredients than I'd ever seen before. It was all very good.

During dinner, we talked about movies and local walking and bike trails, their big brute of a mutt named Bestla, and dogs in general. We never got back to talk of Lucian's work, but after we'd all helped clean up dinner and were standing in the kitchen that looked out over the backyard, Lucian asked me if I'd like to see his lab.

"You have a lab here? In your house?" It was certainly big enough, but still a little surprising.

"Not in the house, out there," he said, nodding toward the dark garden. "Would you like to see it?"

"You might as well go, Perry. He's not going to be happy unless he gets to show you." This from Lily, who said it without sarcasm, but with something more like admiration or pride.

"Sure," I said. "I'd love to."

Lucian walked toward the sliding glass doors to the left of us and hit two switches. Suddenly, the backyard was awash in light. Small ankle-high lamps illuminated the deck, and a string of lights led out to a surprisingly large outbuilding that looked like a tiny house, but that I knew was not.

The backyard was remarkably large, but lots of such a size probably weren't unusual for this older part of Berkeley. Even in the city, some of the stately older homes had similarly spacious gardens. It was wild to see, just the same.

"Wow!" was about all I could think to say.

"I know, right? I never thought I'd have room for a place like this, but thanks to Lily, here we are!"

I turned to Lily, who rolled her eyes in mock embarrassment. "All facilitated by my grandmother. She was born here. Her father built the place, but you know, it got pretty rundown. When she passed, she left the place to me and my brother. He was not enthusiastic about having to renovate or demolish the place, so Lucian worked some magic at the bank, and we bought him out!" Lily explained. "It's been a ten-year labor of love."

"Mostly love," Lucian added, "but sometimes anger and frustration and lots and lots of swearing.

"Wow," I said again. "Very impressive and well worth it, I bet."

"Definitely," they said in unison, and we all laughed as Lucian and I headed out the door and down the garden path.

CHAPTER EIGHT

Drawing up to what looked like a child's playhouse that had morphed from David to Goliath, I paused a minute to take it all in. Not as large as the main house, obviously, but it certainly looked big enough to satisfy thousands of potential renters in the Bay Area. It could have meant a nice passive income stream as well. But no. As I would come to see manifest again and again, Lucian was a man of both ideas and ideals. He would never sink to becoming one of the bourgeoisie — not with a seriously proletariat heart such as his. I would grow to think of him as incorruptible or, at least, in the time I knew him, uncorrupted.

By the time we reached the front door of the fairytale cottage painted in bright red and pale blue, Lucian was as excited as a child showing off a new toy. The doorknob showed golden against the crimson door, as did a set of three additional sturdy and serious locks.

"Listen," Lucian said as he rapped his knuckles against the door.

I raised my eyebrows in surprise.

"Yep," he said. "Solid steel." Lucian lowered his voice to a whisper that may have been facetious but might also have been fully serious. I wasn't sure.

"This place is a fortress," he said. "And it needs to be."

He took out a collection of keys and, after turning the tumblers on four deadbolts, said with a flourish, "Up until this point in the evening, you have been in Kansas." Finally pushing open the door, he added, "Welcome to Oz."

If I had been silently mocking the seriousness and secrecy of Lucian's demeanor, I was no more.

The inside of his dollhouse was outfitted with the kind of equipment I'd only ever seen in the most sophisticated of medical research and treatment facilities. The front was one fairly large room, but I could see there was more space behind a couple of doors beyond the two exam tables. From the outside of the house, well, lab, I had seen two boldly trimmed windows complete with flower boxes. From the inside, I could see those windows were fake. No windows allowed in a fortress. And, of course, it was obvious now why this Oz needed guarding. Even in a quick first evaluation, I noted computers, monitors, microscopes, defibrillators, EEG caps with more electrodes than I'd ever seen before, and, "You've got a portable MRI?"

"Among other things." Lucian smiled.

"I can see that," I said, beginning to wander around.

There were lots of other things. Kind of an unbelievable number of other things. I was truly astonished. And obviously curious. "What exactly did you say you were doing out here, Dr. Frankenstein?"

It was a little mind-boggling and maybe a bit scary to see such a complete lab outside of a medical facility. Lucian and Lily seemed like such nice and normal people, but what did I know? I'd never associated with criminals or spies or whatever was going on here. At least, I didn't think I had. Lucian could see the wheels turning in my mind.

"The perks of working for the government," he explained.

"Which government?" It was only partially a joke.

"The red, white, and blue United States of America," Lucian said with a salute and snap of his heels.

"You would have been more convincing without the boot click," I told him.

"Da, duly noted, comrade," he mocked in a truly terrible Russian accent.

"No, but seriously," I said.

"It's not really a secret. I've published papers. You can find them, I'm sure," he explained. "It's just that it's sensitive and not something anyone outside our specialized community really knows about or thinks about. It's basically brain mapping."

Okay, brain mapping. I understood that, but brain mapping was an ongoing science, something that had been studied for decades. Definitely nothing I could think of that would justify this kind of off-site facility that was built like the Masada, ready to fend off Roman soldiers.

"There's got to be more to it, though, yes?"

"Ah, well, yes. I should have Lily here to explain how this all got started. Maybe we should head back to the house?"

"Sure…"

Now I really was confused. As far as I knew, Lily had no medical training, and having her as a research partner seemed…antithetical to, well…Lily. Maybe she'd been sick at some point? Honestly, I was completely clueless but eager to know more.

Back inside, we joined Bev and Lily in the living room. More wine was poured, and Lucian urged Lily to tell the "story of how all this began." I was literally sitting on the edge of my seat, but Bev was relaxed, looking tired, if not bored. She'd heard the story before, of that, I was sure.

"Okay, are you ready?" Lily asked as if I were about to launch from a zipline and careen down a mountainside. "But first, Bev, let's get you situated. Why don't you go lie down in the bedroom?"

"And miss seeing Perry's face? He's a man of science, you know," Beverly answered.

"Hey! So am I!" Lucian declared with faux consternation.

"You're a scientist…plus," Bev granted. "We'll have to see if Perry can make the leap."

All of this allusion and dancing around whatever it was they were going to tell me was maddening, but I knew they were mostly teasing me, the only member of the group thus far out of the loop.

Before Lily would settle into her story, she had Lucian grab a couple of kitchen chairs and insisted we shift location so that Bev could completely recline on the couch. She fetched a large and puffy bedroom pillow and sat at Bev's feet while Lucian and I took up the wooden chairs. Bestla lounged in front of the couch, and Beverly began mindlessly scratching his massive head.

"Alright then," Lily declared. "So, as you might have guessed, I'm slightly more open-minded and, well, spiritual—for lack of a better word—than my husband here. Yoga opens you up to all kinds of different philosophies and ideas. I started doing a lot of reading and studying and true soul-searching about a dozen or so years ago."

She stopped to gauge my interest and refill my wine glass. I was curious to hear Lily's story, of course, but I'd been through years and years…and years of education, and I was used to this kind of build-up, the kind teachers tried to give new subject matter. The intro—the justification of why we needed to learn such and such a thing—was always the most tedious part. I knew I needed to learn whatever it was to achieve my goals, so just teach it already!

"Okay, so I've had a lot of instructors, and I've studied *a lot* of different philosophies, so when Luce started working with memory specifically, I mentioned that Seth—have you heard of Seth?"

"Seth who?"

Lily laughed.

"Well, that's a good question. See, Seth was an entity channeled by a woman in the sixties and seventies."

"O…kay…" I said slowly. She was losing me for sure, and she could tell.

"Well, a lot of other people have said the same thing since Seth and well, Lucian knows it's true now! Right, honey?"

I was lost. Lucian laughed and nodded his head in the affirmative.

"Lily, Perry has no idea what you're talking about," he said.

Lily regained her composure and took a deep breath. "Okay, so… Seth—and many others before and since of course—talked about all time being simultaneous."

Not a new notion to me. Actually, pretty standard thinking since Einstein. I nodded to signal I got that part.

"Well, listen, Seth talks about using your mind, your imagination, your memory, to revisit the past and literally correct mistakes—change the course of whatever interaction you regret or want to mend or redo or whatever."

"Seems like sound mental-health advice," I granted.

"Right, but you're assuming that it's a 'what if' exercise," Lily corrected me. "As in, 'I wonder what would have happened if I'd chosen to do this or that.' Seth was talking…literally."

"You lost me," I said honestly.

"Look, in physical existence, in any given lifetime…"

Okay, I thought, here we go. Right off the deep end into

reincarnation and psychic readings and fairies and God knows what else. I set my face to semi-smile and half-heartedly urged her to explain further.

"If you will, well, if not accept, at least *consider* the premise of each of us having multiple lifetimes," Lily began again. "But even if you can't accept the idea of reincarnation, just try to consider the idea that within a lifetime, any lifetime, we make millions of little decisions that each have the possibility of changing the trajectory of our existence."

"Okay. Right. That seems pretty straightforward."

"Well, then, consider also the possibility that your soul — the eternal you — has the ability to explore each of those choices. I mean, to actually go off in that direction. It's still you, but also a bit of a different you. Of course, the eternal you, once back in the nonphysical world, can understand and remember the whole of it."

"Are you talking about parallel lives?"

"Yes! Yes! Well, I mean, there is some nuance to it, but that's basically the idea."

"Right," I said. "So, Lucian…you're researching parallel lives?"

"Not exactly."

I laughed because I was still confused and didn't exactly know what I was supposed to say in the face of this weird — and weirdly unsettling — information. What on Earth were they trying to say?

"Someone is going to need to connect the dots, I'm afraid," I finally said.

"Alright, in a nutshell," Lucian began, "I'd been working on brain mapping projects for a number of years and then started concentrating on memory. At first, it was Alzheimer's- and dementia-related, with the intended purpose of helping people reclaim their memories. But then I started to consider other possibilities. And when Lily started talking about everything she was reading in her books, I wondered if there was any semblance of truth to it. And if so, could it be scientifically proven."

Lily took up the story. "Here's the thing. Look around you. This is the here and now. But why is it the here and now?"

She waited for my answer.

"Uh…because…it is?"

"Because it's where our focus is! If we had the ability to completely focus somewhere else — that would be our here and now. Haven't you ever had a smell or a sound wash over you, and for a split second, you're back at the place where you first heard it or smelled it? Haven't you ever felt like the past was right there? Like it still existed, if you could only find a way to get to it?"

"I…I…I mean, yes. I guess," I stammered.

The truth was I knew exactly what she meant. Hadn't I pleaded with the past to give me another chance? Hadn't my dreams taken me back to a place I could see, smell, hear? I tried to hide the slight shudder I felt run through me.

"See? Everyone has. And I thought, well, *Lucian* actually had the brilliant idea that went along with my thoughts and ramblings…like, would it be possible to induce that state?"

I turned to Lucian now. Curious. Skeptical, but definitely curious.

"So, highlight memories? So that they feel real?" I asked.

"So that they *are* real," Lily declared.

I sat back. I wasn't sure if I'd entered Wonderland. Should there have been a "we're all mad here" sign above their front door? In truth, I thought Lucian was probably just exaggerating some success he might have had in some of his research with dementia patients.

"So, you've had success treating Alzheimer's with…memory stimulation?"

"It's not quite that," Lucian said. "And it's well, fairly classified in a kind of nonspecific way. About five years ago, I was approached by some federal officials interested in my work. They specifically asked about treating PTSD in veterans. They talked about suicide among vets and soldiers being unable to return to duty because of PTSD. Could memory-washing—that was their term, not mine—help? So, we started researching. Eventually, they offered me a grant and set me up with what you see outside, and well…it goes on. Now, that aspect of it takes a form more like you described. But, I've also expanded…"

"Expanded?"

"He's refocused people," Lily said bluntly.

It was all a lot to take in, but clearly, we were now at the crux of what was the really important thing. "Refocused?"

"So, it's not exactly time travel…" Lucian began.

"Time travel?" I was alarmed now. What were these two talking about exactly?

"I said not exactly. But with the right tools, anesthetics, and stimuli, it's possible—I mean, I've had success with people actually revisiting their memories. In a literal physical sense. They've changed things. I'm not sure if they've sent things off into a parallel life or not, but when they come back—when I bring them back—they *are* changed. They *are* better."

"This is with PTSD patients?"

"No. With PTSD, we manipulate, erase, or downgrade, if you will, their memories. We fade them in a sense. What I'm telling you about now is…private work. It's experimental but meant to be helpful. The trauma that triggers PTSD is too dangerous to return to at such a real 'you-are-there' level. But imagine being able to literally revisit the past to ease your mind or assuage your grief or figure out a problem…"

"But you're talking about *literally* being there? How do you know it's literal?"

"Ask Lily," he said.

I turned to face her once again.

"I've been back," she said simply.

CHAPTER NINE

Believe me, when I tell you, my friends, I had as many questions as I'm sure you do at this moment. I *will* tell you that we talked for another hour before we realized Beverly had fallen asleep. We all felt awful then about forcing her to try to keep up with us: the younger, the healthier. We woke her gently and helped her to her car. Turned out Ben had been outside patiently waiting the entire time, which I came to understand he was kindly happy to do. We took her home immediately, and Ben and I ushered Beverly inside and, with the help of her nurse, Alicia, to the safety and comfort of her own bed.

She slept, and I pondered the night.

Consider, if you will, the ways in which my life had changed over these few weeks I have thus far revealed to you. My entire world had been picked up, shaken, shattered, spilled forth, and now seemed to be losing its fragile tether to what I thought was a given reality.

So, let me tell you what Lily told me and all that I tried to reassemble in my mind that night after Beverly was tucked safely in bed and the world around me grew quiet.

It seemed Lucian had become fairly obsessed with not only helping people retrace vivid memory but the idea that it might truly be possible to—in a physical sense—revisit the past and perhaps even change it. This notion of focus rang true to him. I understood the concept and agreed that a secure and unwavering focus could make us *feel* like we were truly there when visiting—in dreams or otherwise—an old memory. Again, hadn't I been through it myself? But to make the monumental leap from the idea of mental revelry to an actual physical experience seemed ludicrous…at best.

So when Lily told me the story of her *trip*, I had a mountain of questions, some of which I asked at the time and others of which I held back—not wanting to seem rude or as if I were trying to shatter their hopes and what seemed to me to be illusions.

Lucian explained that at some point, when his research felt constrained by the direction of government officials, he had begun using Lily as a test subject. When I say this, please don't envision daily tests or even dozens of experiments. This was a matter of two total experiments, in which she gladly participated. I could bore you with medical details, but to be honest, it has been a long time since I practiced medicine, and my own memory is not what it used to be. Although, be assured, the facts of my life as I am laying them forth to you are ever vivid and detailed and true. But even the exact science that I do remember would take up time in this memoir that is better spent explaining the experience.

Still, I will tell you the basics as I recall them. Sometime before Lily's adventure, Lucian had put together a four-tiered system of induction into memory. The tiers included using the EEG cap I mentioned seeing in Lucian's lab that first day to stimulate the memory center of the patient's brain. To bring the patient to the specific memory he wanted to reach, the second tier included Lucian leading a type of meditation session (that seemed to me closer to hypnosis) prior to the procedure, wherein the patient was asked to walk through the memory several times. Lucian said this left the memory highlighted to such a degree that it was detectible and, therefore, easier to stimulate electrically once the patient was anesthetized.

Yes, anesthetized. Lucian had experimented with several degrees of mild to moderate monitored sedation that provided the relaxed state needed for patients to successfully reenter a memory. He began by using morphine and then diazepam but found he had the most success with phenobarbital.

Once a patient had gone through the meditation and Lucian had located the area of the brain on which to focus, the patient was lightly sedated. It was at this point Lucian took something of a detour from technology. Yes, he used the skullcap electrodes to send small amounts of electrical current to stimulate the specific portion of the patient's brain that held the specific memory, but then he also used the most basic of co-stimulation devices. Prior to any given experiment, test subjects were asked a series of questions about the memory they were trying to revisit and resolve. Where were you? What was the weather like? What did you smell? And the question that seemed to be most influential: what did you hear? Not human voices, but the other sounds. Traffic, wind, water, music.

Using a simple speaker connected to his phone, Lucian would flood his research shed with those specific sounds, whether they be manmade or natural. Music often brought about the best results, he said.

Did he get results? Oh, yes, both Lily and Lucian declared emphatically. He got them indeed.

As I mentioned, Lucian's PTSD patients were not brought back to memories but rather had them downgraded. This was done mainly by highlighting and making stronger other memories that were more pleasant. Some were from the patients' long-ago past, childhood fun or comfort, for instance. But what seemed to help the most was revisiting pleasant memories closest—linearly speaking—to the trauma itself.

The fact was, Lucian insisted, the treatment was so effective that many patients could be considered cured after only one session.

Lucian told me the story of a young Army soldier who, only a few months out of bootcamp, had tried to thwart but then tragically witnessed the suicide of his friend, a female soldier with whom he had developed an infatuation that he fancied might have been love. True love. The love of his life. The tragedy had so haunted the boy that he couldn't sleep without the help of drugs, became clinically depressed, and nearly stopped eating.

Lucian conducted lengthy pre-session interviews where he collected the data needed for tier four, including the song that had played during the one and only date shared by the ill-fated couple. The pre-induction meditative session included detailing everything the soldier could remember about the good times the two had spent together. And then…all tiers in place, Lucian had electrically stimulated the areas of the brain he said his intricate equipment indicated were holding those good memories. With those memories stimulated, highlighted, and brought to the forefront of his mind, the worst memory slid to the background, where it continued to exist but held less destructive power—overshadowed as it was by the good and pleasant past.

Post-procedure, the boy was not only happier but seemed to be enveloped in a kind of nostalgic bliss related to the enjoyable memories of his fallen friend. In Lucian's words, "The prominence of the good memories overtook the traumatic memory to such an extent that those thoughts were no longer threatening or, in an overall sense, important to the memory of who the young woman was and what she and the boy had shared."

Follow-up with the young soldier had revealed no further sleep issues, a complete alleviation from depression, and an eating pattern perfectly in line with that of a 19-year-old boy. Lucian pronounced him—as did the commanding officers and StratCom—cured.

StratCom—The United States Strategic Command—was the government group funding Lucian's research. Based in Omaha, the organization included eleven unified combat commands, including Armed Forces Intelligence Services. I had looked it all up and read about everything on the StratCom website almost immediately after Lucian told me about his funding. The very idea of this secretive intelligence service conjured up lots of weird *Manchurian Candidate*-type spy scenarios in my mind. After diving into their website, my thoughts didn't change much. I mean, even the name of the place felt like it should always be followed by an exclamation point (Strat-Com!)—like something you'd read about in a comic book. I found the organization frightening and Lucian's association with it…unsettling.

The thing was, despite Lucian's success with his government work, he and Lily couldn't stop thinking about metaphysical theories. The idea of all time being simultaneous and therefore somehow reachable—literally—colored Lucian's success with a stain of *almost*.

That is, they wanted more.

The entirety of Lucian's "more" idea centered around the anesthesia. He figured he'd fairly ironed out the technology of brain mapping and stimulation, so what could bring a patient to that deeper level? It seemed to him quite obvious that unloosing the mind from the present day was the only logical answer. Still, he didn't want to be responsible for crushing a butterfly.

Neither Lucian nor Lily had any idea if there would be repercussions to literally changing the past, that is, revisiting a memory with the express intention of altering it. And because they believed the possibility of doing so was very real, their experimentation seemed concerningly charged with the risk of unintended consequences.

But here, you see, was where Lily's faith in the idea of parallel lives granted them a kind of comfort and maybe even absolution. For, they reasoned, any change they made was only one option in an unknown number of options given to any single moment. Surely, the alteration of a memory was only following through with another possibility that always existed, was it not?

It was all very nebulous and conceptual, and at times, both the Phanes told me they had agreed it might end up proving to be downright silly. Still, they couldn't let it go. Thus, the two continued to search for that perfect, specific incident to alter, and finally, they isolated what they considered a perfect memory.

Lily said she had a short but noticeable scar running across the inside of her right arm. She had gotten in when she was about ten and visiting the very house in which they now lived. Then, it had belonged to her grandmother. The home featured, as it did in the present day, a huge apple tree in the backyard. Lily was forbidden to climb the tree because, her grandmother had explained, if something went wrong, either she or it could be damaged—possibly beyond repair.

Naturally, such an obviously dictatorial adult decree only increased Lily's determination to clamber into the tree's branches in search of forbidden fruit. On this particular summer day, while her grandmother rested, an apple pie they had baked together cooled on the kitchen table, and Billy Joel sang *River of Dreams* on an old console stereo, Lily decided to defy the rules and her own good sense.

She used an overturned terracotta pot to boost herself into the tree, then began to climb, determined to triumphantly return to solid ground with a huge, ripe, and juicy-looking apple she had spotted from below. Unfortunately, her grandma's wisdom proved all too true, and as Lily reached for the apple, she slipped and came crashing down onto the thankfully thick grass below. After a moment, she realized she was fine, except for the gash on her arm. It was about that time she heard her grandmother calling her name.

Knowing her fate if anyone found out about her defiance, Lily slipped undetected into the bathroom off the kitchen and doctored the arm herself, painfully cleaning it by dowsing it with rubbing alcohol. She wrapped it tightly in gauze and snuck into the guestroom to change from her tank top into something with long sleeves, which she wore for the remainder of her visit. (Luckily, not too strange a choice during a cool Berkeley summer.)

So that was it. Specific and well-remembered. Isolated in that only Lily was involved, and only she knew about it. It also included obvious memory cues like the smell of apple pie and a top-40 hit.

It was perfect. The unknowns, then, were two-fold. First, exactly how much phenobarbital should be administered? Phenobarbital was routinely used to induce medical comas in trauma and other cases, so it's side-effects and dosages for various uses were widely known. But, quite obviously, Lucian would be using it in a unique set of circumstances, to say the very least. He decided, wisely, I thought, to err on the side of caution. Later, Lucian said, success had proven his estimation correct.

The second unknown was what exactly would happen if the experiment were successful. What, in fact, did success look like?

"I had this nightmare scenario in my head where we'd be in the middle of the session, and Lily would suddenly disappear," Lucian told me. "Anything seemed possible at that juncture. If we altered history, would history just…take her?"

I'll admit the idea seemed ridiculous to me, but maybe that was only because Lily was so obviously still among us.

Lily said the first try was unsettling because of the intensity of truly reliving the past—actually being there. So, during that first experiment, she didn't try to alter anything but rather, instinctively fought to escape back to the present.

"I knew what was going on," she explained. "I wasn't lost in the memory. I held the understanding of my present life and the experiment—although I simultaneously looked and felt to be my ten-year-old self—but I sensed how easy it would be to get lost in yesterday, and I suddenly panicked. It felt like I was drowning in my own past, and I desperately needed a gulp of the present. I wanted my reality back. What felt to me like fighting my way home looked to Lucian like terror at best and heart issues at worst, so he brought me out of it pretty quickly."

According to both Lucian and Lily, every bit of that first try was upsetting, so they put aside the idea and any more experimentation… for a while. But then, Lily said, she just couldn't resist. The lure of the past was too great. They tried again a couple of weeks later, and this time, Lucian increased the dosage of phenol to nearly the levels of an induced coma.

Hearing those words highlighted what seemed to me the complete recklessness of these wild experiments and brought to mind the Gatsby discussion Beverly and I'd had. One of the book's most famous scenes and often quoted lines came rushing back to my mind, and I wondered, were Lily and Lucian like that? Careless? Did they smash things up and then…retreat?

So many emotions and so many questions. A lot of judgement, to be sure, but also—in the very back of my mind, somewhere among my nightmares, I recognized something like…possibility that might even lead to…hope?

The second experiment found Lily again completely immersed in her memory. She touched the tree, she said. Felt the sun. Ran up to the terracotta planter with glee. She could smell the apple pie resting on the kitchen table and even ventured a glance into the bedroom, where her grandmother—very much alive and well—lay resting. It was all real, she claimed. It was joyous and exhilarating and completely intertwined with her ability to understand that she was there on leave. She remembered the task at hand and so grabbed the pot, stood upon it, and then…waited. Just waited, basking in the reality of her life more than 20 years prior. Lily and Lucian had tried to figure out the timing. How long was it from the retrieving of the flowerpot until Lily's grandmother had called her name? They figured no more than ten minutes, and that was exactly how long Lucian allowed Lily to stay in the immersive state.

Yet, in one of the possibilities they hadn't considered, the time felt considerably longer to Lily. She estimated she was dwelling in her own past for close to an hour, perhaps longer. Neither Lucian, with his science nor Lily, with her pseudoscience, had a solid explanation for that structural difference, that bending of time. Still, it turned out to be such an overall successful experiment that Lucian was thrilled and ready to simply celebrate. Lily admitted it took her longer, perhaps obviously, to recover from this deep, personal experience, but she never wavered in her conviction of the truth of it all. She had, she told me, been there, lived it—relived it literally.

I humored them in their seriousness, but it all seemed wildly speculative, to say the least. Had I not just spent the evening with their intellectual, articulate, gracious, and rational selves, I would have dismissed all of it as a complete fairytale.

But then, as if reading my mind, Lily raised her right arm and lifted the sleeve of her long, colorful dress. She twisted it so that I could see the soft, white inner side. I looked up at her, questioning.

"No scar," was all she said.

CHAPTER TEN

Before falling asleep, Bebe had offered, and I accepted, an invitation to stay at her house that night. Ben surely would have driven me home, but I was weary from wine and talk and worried too—as was coming to be something of a norm for me—about Beverly. I took the guestroom to the left of Bev's own, as Alicia occupied an adjoining suite to the right. Alicia's room was also hooked to a kind of baby monitor surveillance system, giving her the ability to check on Bev 24-7. I asked her to please let me know if Bev needed anything or if there were any problems. I pressed upon her the fact that I was, after all, an oncologist and well aware of the precariousness of Ms. Bowen's health as well as any issues or complications that might arise.

The fact that I was a doctor went a long way in mollifying any doubts either Ben or Alicia might have had about the nature of our relationship. My M.D. seemed to assure them both that I was neither gigolo nor conman. As a physician constantly surrounded by other physicians, I knew that my degree absolutely did not preclude me from lies or hucksterism. I understood Jesus's admonition for physicians to "heal thyself" because I'd see how often my fellow doctors needed healing in many, many different areas of their lives, our lives.

But their trust in me led me to wonder — that night especially — whether or not I held that same faith in myself. Who was I to act as if I were impervious to the…well, desires of the flesh, so to speak? What I felt for Beverly was so close and so complete. It lit me from within but also connected me to her in a way I had never experienced before and, in fact, had never really believed possible. And if we didn't exactly embody the teenaged infatuation of Romeo and Juliet, there was, nevertheless, an intensity that revolved around and ran through us to such an urgent degree that I couldn't help but mourn or even keen over the innumerable small cruelties of this disease and curse of timing.

But then, what was time? Lily and Lucian were forcing me to confront and question everything I'd previously known as basic, linear reality. I could feel the walls in my well-constructed certainty beginning to crack and shudder. And what were walls anyway, once you understood the fragility of the foundation on which they were built?

Beverly was up before me the next morning, and we spent the day together, being gentle with the vulnerability of our newly discovered selves. That is to say; we talked in the cool and breezy sunshine about things we loved and the people who made us happy. Again and again, we fell upon each other's words with what seemed like practiced, theatrical timing that, by the end of the day, felt almost comical. Along with a psychic's worth of I-was-just-going-to-say-that's, we also found ourselves quite literally finishing each other's sentences. It might have been unnerving had it not been so easy to fall into the patterns of an old married couple. It felt as if we'd spent a lifetime together. And who knows? Maybe we had.

In the evening, over a dinner ordered from a favorite spot of Bev's, we finally broached the subject of Lily and Lucian and what they were doing…or what they thought they were doing.

"So…the scar, no scar thing…you know about that, right?" I asked.

"Yes, of course. Lily couldn't keep it to herself; she was so elated. Lucian too. More proud than elated, though, I think."

I didn't want to come off as condescending or doubting, but I barely knew the Phanes and certainly didn't know what to make of their experiments. "It's a lot to take in…to consider. I keep trying to think of plot holes."

"I did the same thing!" Bev said as she laughed her pure laugh.

"Lily's talk about parallel lives…I mean, does her not having a scar now mean she shifted to a parallel life? Are we a part of that parallel life? But, if so, I mean, if she changed history, even her history, how does Lucian remember the scar?"

"Lucian and I."

"You remember it too? Seriously?"

"She showed it to me the day before. She said, without context at all, 'I want you to remember this scar.' I thought she was going to give me some profound bit of metaphysical wisdom about scars and healing in our lives."

"And?"

"And she didn't. Well, actually, maybe she did because I remember the scar, and now it's gone."

"Healed," I offered.

"Not healed," Bev said. "Erased."

The evening lingered on, but soon enough, I knew that I needed to get home. I'd worn the same clothes for two days, and I had to be at the clinic early the next morning. Mondays were always hectic. And Bev, of course, required rest. She had another week before her next infusion and needed to gain as much strength as possible during that time. I thought her attitude and resilience quite remarkable, and told her so several times. Finally, though, she asked Ben to bring the car around to take me to the Hines' house, where I'd left my own vehicle the day of the shower.

Bev walked me slowly to the front foyer of the house, and we lingered in the doorway. After I told her I hoped to see her again soon, I stood trying to form the next sentence but became lost in a thousand possibilities, none of them adequate. I took her hand. It was soft and thin, strong at the moment but threatening frailty. I could see the whisps of hair under her scarf, the wrinkles around her eyes, the weight and wonder of more than sixty years well-lived, and to me, all of it was beautiful.

I leaned in toward her, and she whispered a cautionary, "Perry…"

But I was without caution or care and entangled in the very essence of her and me and every parallel life we might have ever lived or ever would. I kissed her gently at first but then with a passion that seemed instantly quenched and forever unquenchable. When our lips finally parted, we stood, foreheads touching, and sighed heavy sighs together.

We laughed at that and said nothing more. The words that needed to be expressed and all the entanglements and wonder that came with them were too much to unloose at that moment. I understood that both she and I needed to sort through, perhaps dissect, and definitely reflect on the past two days. I was exhilarated and exhausted, and after sitting for a while in the luxury of Beverly's black Mercedes, my mind fell back into another line from *The Great Gatsby*. And it became so loud and so deep that I was afraid I might fairly drown in it.

"So we drove on," Fitzgerald had written, "toward death through the cooling twilight."

• • •

I never failed to appreciate my education or my career and all the benefits it afforded me, both material and deferential. But that Monday morning, for the first time, I felt my job as an actual relief. It was comforting to have something solid and routine to occupy my time and thoughts. I'd reasoned and rationalized far too much over the course of our protracted weekend, and it seemed unnecessarily exhausting to keep taxing my brain—as well as my heart…and maybe my soul—any longer.

I knew there would be questions from both Samay and Victoire, the former because I knew he'd seen me exit the shower with Beverly and the latter because I'd left my car so long at her parents' house. But I welcomed that too. Those would be awkward but navigable conversations. I would, I thought, be able to converse with little effort and fall back into easy comradery without confusion.

Samay found me first. Coming up from behind, he caught me by the elbow and dragged me from corridor to corner where we had a modicum of privacy.

"Dude, what the hell happened to you this weekend? I texted, like, fifty times and even called!"

Voice communication was the height of desperation for Samay.

"I know man, I'm sorry. I meant to get back to you. I was just so tired when I finally got home last night."

"Last night? Finally got home *last night*? What happened? Did that old lady die?"

"No! God no, Samay! What the hell?"

"Sorry! Geeze, man. Don't bite my head off! I just saw you leave with her, and I know she's that cancer lady, and she looked…well, not that great. What's going on with you?"

"Nothing!"

And I knew I "doth protest too much" once again as soon as the word came out of my mouth. This wasn't a familiar or easy conversation after all. And as much as I liked Samay and had a lot of fun with our usual banter, this was definitely not that, and I wanted to be done.

"Look. I'm sorry. I guess I'm still tired. Beverly is fine. Everyone is fine. I'm fine. You fine?"

"I'm fine, Perry. But I'm serious now, are you all right? Really, like, okay?"

I considered for a moment — just a moment — the idea of spilling everything — Beverly and me and my feelings and Lily and Lucian and their crazy theories and experiments — all of it. But the weight of it was too much to lift out of my body and into the hallway to tumble over Samay and linger in the air and then fall loose and exposed on the tile. It was hard enough having it in me. I couldn't risk stepping on it and through it all day.

"I'm fine, really. Maybe it's just the whole thing with watching Vic and Michael so happy and the baby and everyone being together again, you know?"

I lied and told the truth at the same time. But I figured it would be enough for Samay to latch on to while also keeping him (he of the "why would I want to talk about my feelings?" school of thought) at bay.

"Yeah, yeah, I get that. It was all kind of weird, surreal even. But it's good too, right? You're happy for them, aren't you?"

"Yeah. Yes. Of course. It was just a lot all at once."

Now that we were venturing into deeper meanings and — God forbid — feelings, Samay was anxious to be on his way. And this time, it was what I wanted too.

"Alright, well, just checking in. But if you're all good, maybe I'll just see you later? Maybe I'll do the game this week? Or remind me to tell you what my dad's got going on next weekend. He keeps bugging me about it, and you know what that means…"

"I'm getting bugged too. Got it."

I was used to being a buffer between Samay and Mr. Shankar. I liked them both, so it was no burden. I couldn't begin to count the many times Mr. Shankar had begun a sentence with, "Tell my stubborn son…" or "Tell my know-it-all son…" while Samay stood beside me in the same room. For his part, Samay would grow exasperated, and, on the verge of outright defiance, he would give me *the look*. That was my cue to change the subject (Did I tell you about the new Indian restaurant near campus?) or say something funny (not easy) or self-deprecating (easy). All in all, I envied the relationship Samay had with his father, and I felt a kind of desperation to make sure they stayed on an even keel.

"Don't take your parents for granted," I'd told Samay often, perhaps too often.

That day, our three-cornered relationship came in handy. It brought us back from a strange and prickly place to one of routine and common understanding. We got back on a familiar footing.

I'd taken off early Friday and now faced the busy Monday morning backlash to that early exit and a weekend off. It was all good. I was happy to be distracted. When I got ready to leave late in the afternoon—evening really—Victoire finally caught up with me. She'd been trying to touch base all day, she said.

"You left before I could say a real goodbye on Saturday."

"I know, I'm sorry. So many people surrounding the center of attention."

I nodded at her pregnant belly. She laughed and assured me she understood. Turned out she just wanted to let me know that she was starting her maternity leave a little earlier than she'd previously told me. That very day, in fact.

I offered my congratulations for both her wisdom and freedom, although I wasn't sure those were quite the right words. But she didn't question them. Victoire had come a long way since our harried and innocent med-school days, and all the time she spent nurturing me throughout our very lopsided time together. Vic had given more than any partner should have to give in a relationship. I'd truly meant to be reciprocal, but things always weighed heavily on the side of me…my needs…my issues…my problems. I'd thought about our relationship and its dreary demise long and often. Finally, I'd come to understand that although I had loved Victoire with a ferocity, I needed her—and perhaps used her—even more.

Vic—patient, kind, smart, insightful, Vic—deserved so much more, and I believed she had found it in Michael. Of course, that meant I had lost it, but sometimes losses are deserved. And sometimes, a win is as simple as turning away from the things that hurt us and turning toward something that is painless.

Victoire laughed a bit as we hugged.

"I'll take congratulations, I guess," she said.

"I hope you know that it means I'm happy for you. You know that, right? I'm really happy for you," I said sincerely as a lump formed in my throat.

How strange to get choked up over such a statement while standing in a hospital hallway. The same place where I spent my long and singularly focused days and where the sick and infirm trundled alongside the volunteers and us, the would-be healers. But I could see Victoire's life laid out before her in a technicolor brilliance that had always escaped our own plans and dreams. Michael and Victoire with fulfilling careers, beautiful home, two children, maybe more. Surrounded by family, basking in change of the best kind, first steps and birthdays, holiday traditions, and the promise of *I am here for you.*

God, how self-absorbed and blind I'd been.

I'd hoped that day would bring a refreshing pool of familiar tasks and the distraction of hard work. But it had devolved into the troubled waters of unknown emotion. I'd had enough of that over the weekend. In fact, I was exhausted by it. I hugged Victoire again, wished her the best, and said I was sorry but had work; there was so much to catch up on and all that. I'd been about to walk out of the hospital, but now I turned toward my office. Of course, there was work I could take on, focus that would then be demanded. But as soon as I got to the safety of my own desk and computer, I could only slump into my chair and stare at the UCSF screensaver that bounced across the monitor. I tried to stop my dizzying thoughts from landing on those things that most confounded and frightened me.

Still, the Universe has a way of making us face ourselves again and again. Painful, yes. But what is life if not a relentless dance with pain? My door was slightly ajar when I heard a gentle tap.

"Knock-knock. Hi there. Just thought I'd check in on my favorite patient or maybe just say hi to a friend?"

"Oh, Lien. I should have rescheduled our appointment. I'm sorry."

"Or just say hi?" she offered again.

"Or just say hi. You're right. I'm sorry, times two."

"No need to apologize. I was just thinking about you. Then I thought, why not drop by and see if you were around and maybe up for a visit…or a talk?"

"Or a little therapy?"

"Hey, whatever you need. I hope you know that."

"I do."

And I did. Still, where to begin? And should I begin? But in the end, I knew Lien's professional ethics — hadn't I already run into them? — and I knew without a doubt that anything I said would be kept in complete and utter professional confidence. I also understood she would weigh anything I said on an educated and caring scale.

And so, I unburdened myself and told her everything. I told her about Bev and my feelings and the weekend and the myriad of strange coincidences that felt like anything but, and I explained about Lily and Lucian and everything that had thus far come from knowing them, and I even spoke of that very day with Samay and Victoire. After an hour, I felt lighter and relieved but spent.

"No more questions? So, you're ready to render a diagnosis?"

It was a joke…if she wanted it to be.

"Perry," she began, "throughout this…session…you've been answering your own questions."

"Have I?"

"You drew the parallel yourself. You noted Beverly's age and her illness. You talked of the cessation of dreams about your mother. You see what's going on here, correct? Even that strange connection you talked about. Who are you really connecting to, do you think, Perry?"

She was right in one sense. Of course, I had thought about projection and the Oedipal implications. It was the most obvious, the clearest explanation for my attraction to Beverly. She was nearly my mother's age or the age she would have been. She was suffering from the same disease, which meant she offered me the promise of a kind of redemption…if I could stay. If I could be there for her at the end.

Yes, I'd gone over these things again and again and knew the obviousness of the situation would color the lens through which all my friends and colleagues would likely view us. So, in that sense, yes, she was right. And yet, I knew it wasn't the truth. Not the full truth. I thanked Lien. Told her I'd talk to her again soon. Assured her she'd helped and that I would think about everything she'd said to me.

But when she left, and I was again in front of my computer — staring — that phrase ran through and looped around my mind, and yet. And yet. And yet.

And yet, I understood what I felt with a certainty that defied analysis. I'd felt it in every moment I'd spent with Beverly since the day we met. I felt it in every conversation we'd had, every laugh we'd shared. I knew it in the kiss. The coincidences between her and my mother were many, but they were just that. Or, and I considered this for a long moment, maybe life really was more like Lily would have me believe. Maybe these weren't coincidences. Maybe everything about and around and connecting me to Bev had a purpose. And maybe that purpose had something to do with opportunity, a chance to do better, perhaps, as Lien suspected. But maybe it was as simple as a chance to love, to love truly and deeply and without question. And everyone deserved a chance to love, didn't they?

CHAPTER ELEVEN

The truth of knowing what my relationship with Beverly wasn't, suddenly made me aware and sure of what it was. I sat with the knowledge for a long time. I let it take shape and escape into the air around me, where it condensed and fell like rain. It was everywhere, and it soaked me to the skin.

I stayed in my office much later than usual that evening. I needed the time to let my evolution catch up to me. I knew, obviously, that I needed to see Beverly again — speak to her, touch her — but I needed first to fully recognize what I was feeling and where I was willing to go with it. Had I not lingered in my thoughts so long, Samay might not have caught up with me, and perhaps everything would have taken a very different path. Who knows?

As it was, I heard my name ringing through the parking lot just as I was about to get into my car and drive home. Samay's voice boomed and echoed through the underground garage like the voice of God.

"Oh man, I'm glad I caught you. Look, I need you to do me a huge favor. Will you?"

It could only be bad if he led with the question before even telling me what was being asked. "I mean…if I can…"

"It's nothing bad. It's not even that hard. It's like…I just don't want to do it alone, you know?"

"I actually don't know. But I'm listening."

"It's my dad. Remember, I kind of told you? I mean, you know my dad. It's one of his things. One of his India things, and my mother says I'm absolutely duty-bound to go. It's not awful if you're there, but it is if I'm alone with all of them."

"All of who?"

"My parents, my family. I mean, *all* of my family. Half of India, dude. It's kind of a big deal."

"Still not sure what it is we're talking about…"

"Okay, you know my dad's a promotor…"

"He what?"

"So, maybe you don't know. Sorry. It's like one of the things he does. It's not like he's selling out Levi Stadium or something. It's for the Indian community around here. Festivals and lectures, concerts, and what have you. Well, Saturday, he's got a concert going on in Golden Gate Park. There's half a dozen groups, dancers, musicians, whatever. There's going to be a sitar thing that's a tribute to Ravi Shankar — so you can see why he's so gung-ho about it, right? Anyway, will you come? I'll bring the beer. And food. Or pay for food or whatever they have. Will you come? Help me please, Obi-Wan. You're my only hope!"

It didn't sound awful to me. In fact, the very idea of being surrounded by immediate and extended family in any sort of situation always seemed to me completely not awful. But something he'd mentioned was still vibrating through me.

"Can I bring someone?"

"Dude, bring anyone and everyone. I'm trying to get Mike and Vic to come. She said she'll see how she feels. You bring a date. I might try to find one myself. I just didn't want to ask someone new and then bore them to death, you know?"

"Yeah, okay. I can make it. I'll let you know if there's a plus-one."

"Oh man, you don't know how much I appreciate this! I'll get all the details, and we'll make plans sometime later this week."

"Sounds good."

"And you won't back out now…promise?"

"I won't, and I promise."

Samay took my promise and bolted before I had a chance to renege or make any demands on his time at all. I sat in my car and smiled. Of course, I'd instantly thought of Bebe and the offer to play her Ravi Shankar album for me. How much better was this opportunity to discover his music—or his type of music—together on a beautiful day in the park?

Since the weekend and my experiences with Beverly, I'd felt time shrinking around me. I knew the likelihood of Beverly ever getting better was so slim as to be nearly nonexistent. And the urgency I felt to have her near made caring about what others might think immaterial. My feelings for Bev were as serious and entrenched as her vicious disease—with just as little chance for recovery.

I called Bev from my car then, eager to share the idea—ask her to go with me and have her say yes—so that possibility was settled into a promise. She was, happily, just as enthusiastic as I was and asked if I would mind if she invited Lily and Lucian.

The concert was open to the public, and I was happy to let Lucian and Lily and Victoire and Samay and the whole damned world see Bebe and I together. Surely, if the memories of a thousand people held us—Bev and I—in their minds, the truth of we two would be established, solid. I welcomed all eyes because they might possibly amplify my own vision.

After the call, I sat satisfied in my car for a moment. I was ready to be home now. Happy and replete with anticipation. But then I thought of something. I made another phone call. It rang twice before she picked up. I was overly eager and spoke immediately as if in the middle of a conversation already.

"What are you doing this weekend?"

"What? Perry? Is that you?"

"Yes, it's me. I'm asking what you're doing this weekend because I want you to see something; well, someone and something."

"What are you talking about?"

"I'm sorry." I laughed, suddenly realizing I was sounding a bit crazy. "Look, Lien, there's a concert in the park this weekend. My friend Samay—Dr. Shankar—do you know him? Anyway, his father is promoting it. It's an Indian cultural thing: concerts, food, etc. A few friends are going, Michael and Victoire Hines—I know you know them—and…I invited Beverly Bowen."

Silence on the other end of the phone. But I knew I'd spoken in a fast and jumbled blur. So maybe Lien just needed a minute to decipher it all.

"And…you're asking me to go as a friend? Or as your therapist?"

"Well, both, maybe?"

"Perry, I…"

"No, wait. As a friend. Really. I'm not looking for analysis, but I would like you to see us together or maybe just be with us together."

"So, you want me there as a friend…not to prove something to your therapist? Validation of some sort?"

I had to stop and think for a minute. Not because I didn't know that answer but because—as so often the case these days—it was such an arduous task to articulate feelings that were outside the realm of mere words.

"Not in the sense you think. And validation isn't exactly the right word. I just want everyone to know Bev and I as an 'us.' And I want everyone I know and love to share a few of our moments together so the memory of us is…sturdier…"

"Perry, I…"

"Please come, Lien. Please say you'll help me hold this memory. From your point of view, of course. Your honest point of view."

"The gospel according to Lien?"

It was a subtle joke, I knew. But to me, it seemed apt. I knew I'd need this Good Book in the future.

"Exactly," I said.

She breathed in deeply, and I heard her sigh. A slight sigh. The kind she tried to hide in her office. A kind of dismay.

"Alright," she said finally. "Send me the details. I'll be there."

Everything was set, and I was euphoric. I could go home now and rest, sleep with the satisfaction of knowing there was something to wake up for. The best sleep comes from the promise of sharing the next day with someone you love. *Love.* I turned the word around in my head, seeing it clearly from all angles for the first time.

I smiled.

When I called Beverly the next day, she was even more enthusiastic about the concert than the night before. She had already talked to Lily and secured her promise to attend. Bev mentioned too how nice it would be to get to know Kabir and Hema better and said she looked forward to seeing everyone else again. I explained that Lien would also be there, and we had a long discussion about her role as both friend and therapist and my need for therapy in general. I had touched on it before, but now I felt I could—should—tell her everything.

"And Lien, Dr. Tran, you've told her about…us?"

I smiled into my phone. It was nice to hear Bebe say 'us.' It felt conspiratorial but also like a declaration.

"Yes. I'm sorry. Maybe I should have asked?"

"Don't be silly. I don't even have the right to question you. Therapy is—and should be—private. Personal. It just popped out. I mean, because she'll only be there as a friend. A friend, yes?"

"Definitely as a friend. I had to reassure her of the same thing."

Beverly was silent for a minute. In the same way Lien had been silent. They both saw me better than I saw myself.

"She didn't happen to mention the name Oedipus in therapy, did she?" Bev finally asked.

"Hmmm. What was that name again? Opie? Eppi…Epple…"

She laughed. A good, solid, throw-your-head-back kind of laugh. Then I laughed because, of course. Of course, we both understood what others, maybe everyone, might think. Obviously, it wasn't anything either of us hadn't already thought of ourselves.

And the laugh we shared wasn't that of a thief's guilty denial. Rather, it was an honest guffaw because, like comedians ahead of our time, we knew that even if everyone else misunderstood, ours was still a great joke.

The only possible glitch with our Saturday plans was the timing of Bev's next infusion, which was scheduled for the following day, Wednesday. Generally, we tell patients they'll likely feel pretty good the day of their chemo and often the day after as well. The third day is the one that tends to bear the full weight of everything their body is going through, taking in, and fighting off.

Saturday would be the fourth day, perhaps much better, but perhaps not. The fourth day was often still difficult. In fact, there was nothing in the cancer playbook that guaranteed wins and losses. Far from it. Cancer was nothing if not capricious. It had no problem lying and often teased with promises it never meant to keep. It could be cruel in the worst ways and oblivious to its own mercilessness. The relentless nature of cancer — all cancer — was why there was such joy when we triumphed, even in small ways and even if the celebration was short-lived. Every battle — every skirmish — was hard-fought, and patients, doctors, family, and friends reveled in all victories, whether huge or minute.

We planned that Lily, Lucian, and I would all meet at Bev's on Saturday morning. If she felt up to going, we'd all work to make preparation and transportation as easy and painless as possible for Beverly. If she was having a bad day, we'd stay home with her and try to do the same.

"Keep watch when I'm asleep and make me laugh when I'm awake," was all Beverly said she would ever ask of us.

If she did end up feeling well enough to go, we wouldn't have to worry about finding a rare parking space and walking who knows how far. Bev's driver could take us to one of the designated drop-off locations that were close to the amphitheater and to plenty of seating. Ben, I knew, would help us in any way he could and be there when we were ready to go home. Money really did have its perks.

"I can call Lily and let them know," Bebe said. Then there was silence.

"Beverly? Are you still there?" I asked, instantly concerned, nervous.

"You know…" she began slowly, and I knew she'd been considering whether or not to say the something she was about to say. "I've been thinking about your dreams…about all of that last day…your mother… I was thinking perhaps Saturday would be a good time for you to have a nice, long talk with Lucian. Maybe he could help."

CHAPTER TWELVE

There's a kind of loop that surrounds the music concourse in Golden Gate Park. It's a walkable oval — an easy, paved path — that travels from the band shell at one end to the giant Ferris wheel at the other. Near both are drop-off points meant to provide simple access for those who want to get to specific areas within the thousand-plus acre park that covers more than three miles.

Ben dropped us close to the amphitheater, where I promised there would be plenty of benches. Even from the car, we could see the area was full of food, crafts, and various Indian-culture-related booths surrounded by hundreds of people. Ben helped us — and especially Beverly, of course — exit the car, and as our entourage began walking, we caught sight of Samay and his parents almost immediately. They were standing near the half-shell where musical groups were already gathering, getting ready to perform.

We waved and walked up slowly. Beverly said she was feeling fine, but I didn't want to tax her unnecessarily, and we were all happy to take a leisurely pace anyway, talking as we were and getting to know ourselves as a group of new friends. Just as we came up next to the Shankars, I heard my name.

"Perry!"

Lien was walking at a brisk pace from the direction of the Sky-Star Wheel, waving her hand to flag us down. We all waited as she quickly made her way to us.

"And here I was afraid I wouldn't be able to find you!"

"We just got here, so…perfect timing, I guess!" I said, then provided introductions. "Lien, these are my friends Beverly, Lily, and her husband Lucian. Everybody, this is my friend Lien. We work together at the hospital."

"You're a doctor too, I suppose?" Lily asked.

"Yes," Lien said. "Psychiatrist."

"Well, here we are again, Bev, the only two non-doctors in the group!" Lily joked.

"I don't know," Bev teased. "The hospital is my second home these days. You'd think I'd be due for an honorary something or other."

"This way then, Dr. Bowen," I said grandly with a sweep of my arm.

"Well, fine, I just guess I'll be the only normal one in the group then," Lily said. She was teasing, I knew, but she might have been right.

By the time those initial introductions were done, Victoire, Michael, and Vic's parents had also arrived. Bev and Hema began talking about the upcoming music, with Beverly reminiscing about how Ravi Shankar and someone called Sadji Kahn had been all the rage during the sixties or maybe seventies. It was apparently an odd pop-culture juncture that included Nehru jackets, teenaged Indian heartthrobs, and sitar music. Bev wouldn't have quite been a teenager then but later explained to me that her nannies, drivers, and other household staff were the people with whom she spent the most time after her mother died. Their likes and tastes colored her world like an invitation to a ball she could envision but never attend. Bev said she always longed to be a peer and not a charge.

I didn't—couldn't—add much to the conversation. But I loved listening to Bebe talk with so much animation. I couldn't help but smile just watching her reminisce with Hema and chat with Kabir. It was a joy to see her talk and smile and laugh. It made me happy to see others listening to her and enjoying her company. I felt a silent camaraderie with them because I could see they, too, were happy to be around her.

The others—my own peers—had mostly wandered off by then, some getting food. Lucian was sent on a mission to find us good seats. I too stepped back a bit to be alone and gain a better vantage point of the entire scene, with Beverly at its center. But after a while, Lily was at my side.

"She's something, isn't she," Lily said in the form of a declaration, not a question.

"She is that."

"She's pretty taken with you, you know."

"Is she?" I asked as I continued to watch her. "I hope so."

"Yes. I thought you would."

I steered my eyes away from Beverly to take a serious look at Lily. There seemed no questions or judgement in her eyes. "It's hard to explain. I don't quite understand it myself."

"When you've lived your life almost completely in the physical, it can be unsettling to suddenly be in touch with the nonphysical. Your soul-self," Lily said without a touch of humor or teasing.

I didn't consider myself a cynical person, and heaven knew since my mother's death, I'd thought a lot—too much, many would say—about the possibility of life after death, heaven, hell, what my life might mean—or any life might mean— if I could rely on it being only a fraction of eternity. Still, this kind of easy acceptance of something I was not quite ready to declare real would normally have made me uncomfortable or even struck me as naïve or ridiculous. But I held onto Lily's soft gaze and felt a kind of relief at an explanation that seemed gently plausible.

"Yes," I finally said. "But it feels…right. It makes me happy. Calm."

"Of course it does!" she said, becoming suddenly enthusiastic. "You're finally back in touch with the truest, deepest part of you!" Then, she grew serious and quiet. "And Bebe is too. I can see it. I can feel it."

Lily and I then walked back over to where groups of our friends stood talking in a couple of different conversations. I came up to Bebe's side and just listened. Smiled. After a while, I had that feeling you get when you know someone is watching you, and I turned to see the eyes of Samay and Lien on both of us. Wondering.

I'd like to say how much I enjoyed the concert, and there were parts of it I liked very much, but in truth it was…lengthy. Along with the sitar concerto—featuring a group of more than a dozen players—there was other music and singing and dance provided by performers of varying ages. The youngest of the belly dancers were probably only five or six. Cute. But again, long.

Food and craft booths stayed open after the show part of the day was over, but everything started to break up pretty quickly after the last act. We said our goodbyes to Hema and Kabir, as well as Michael and Victoire. Vic managed to whisper to me as they were leaving that she was going to call me soon because we "need to talk."

That was fine. Let the world talk to me—say whatever it would—it didn't matter. I didn't care. I thought it was probably time for us to get going too. But Bebe had different ideas.

"Let's go ride the SkyStar," she said. "I've never been on, and I don't want to miss my chance."

For a second, those words struck my heart, but then I realized she simply could have been referring to the fact that the giant Ferris wheel's installation was temporary—its time in San Francisco was slated to end soon, not that her life was the same.

Everyone was more enthusiastic than I, including Lien and Samay. Though the idea sounded fun, I worried about the walk—the SkyStar was behind the Francis Scott Key Monument at the opposite end of the music concourse from where we stood. It was a long walk. And I feared it might be too much Beverly.

"You're not afraid of heights, are you?" Bev teased me.

"Me? Afraid of heights? I'll have you know I ride the elevator at work to the fourth floor every single day."

Everyone *oohed* and *ahhed* with sarcastic admiration, and we all laughed. I wanted Bev to be safe and resting at home, but I also didn't want the afternoon to end. So off we went at as slow a pace as I could set without seeming overly solicitous. Everyone saw through me though of course.

Because it had been her idea, Beverly wanted to pay for everyone, and though we all balked, she insisted, and we acquiesced fairly quickly. She wanted us all to ride on the VIP gondola, but it only seated five, and we were a half-dozen.

All six could have fit in one of the regular carriages, but Lily spoke up. "Why should you have to skip the VIP experience?" she asked Bev. "C'mon. You deserve it. Why don't you and Perry take the VIP trip, and the rest of us will mingle with the peasants? We don't mind, do we?"

"I'm not ashamed to say I belong with the peasants," Samay assured us.

"Well, what do you say, Dr. Roberts? VIP treatment?" Bev asked me.

"I would absolutely settle for nothing less, my dear."

It was my best attempt at an upper-crust English accent, but it might have fallen short. Everyone thought it was hilarious.

"Ahhhh, whatta youse guys know anyhows?" I shot back.

"Oh my God, dude, and I thought your English accent was bad. All of New York is crying right now!"

Trust Samay. But it was fine. It was all fine.

The VIP gondola had leather seats and a generally plush interior. We ended up boarding before the others got into their slightly-less-plush cabin, but our trip was a few minutes longer, as befitted VIPs.

Bev sighed as she sat down, and I was worried. It had been too long a walk, too long a day. She looked very tired. Beautiful, but tired. I asked if she was okay, and Bev assured me she was fine and "ready to ride to heaven," which I thought a very poor choice of words. But then we were quickly high above the city, able to see everything in vivid color, from the blue of the bay to the orange of the Golden Gate Bridge. The sun was getting ready to slide into the water, and at that moment, the hope and possibility of love and everything it touched swelled in my heart, and maybe my soul, and my eyes grew glassy.

"It makes you want to cry, doesn't it?" Beverly's own eyes were welling up, and I leaned over to hold her tightly and kiss her forehead.

"Do you think you can capture moments?" I asked.

"That's what pictures are for."

"No. I mean, grab one and hold onto it so tightly that it's embedded? Embedded in your heart and your brain and your soul. You know, so you can always go back to it when you need to."

"Now you sound like Lucian."

It was true. Now I sounded like Lucian.

"Do you know what this reminds me of?" Bev asked.

"Icarus?" I answered.

"Oh dear. I hope not!" She said with a laughed. "No. It reminds me of one summer right after I graduated college. My dad was still alive and anxious for me to join the company. But I was so defiant! I was determined to make my own way. Do what I wanted to do. On my own, dammit!" She laughed at the memory.

"So, what was it you were so determined to do?"

"I had no idea! But I had a couple of friends who had gotten jobs at Great America. It hadn't been open very long, and supposedly, it was a wonderful place to work and an especially great place to meet cute guys."

"Cute guys who worked at an amusement park? Stellar prospects there."

"True enough. But none of us thought much about mapping out a reliable future. We weren't looking for husbands. We were just looking for…you know…summer fun."

"Mmm, I bet."

She laughed at that; literally threw her head back and laughed in that way she had. I looked at all of her: cast and thinning hair hidden by her scarf, crow's feet, perfectly coordinated clothing, and sparkling gold earrings. And as I breathed in her delicate perfume, I could see through this beautiful "now" self to the 22- or 23-year-old Beverly, eager to prove herself, eager to have some fun, with no idea how soon her father would be gone and how soon her entire world would change.

Bev talked about being high above Santa Clara on Great America's three-armed Ferris wheel called the Sky Whirl. I too had ridden in one of its cages as a very young child, perhaps a year before it was removed. An icon of the park and its beginning, now permanently and sadly gone forever.

Actually, I'd been to Great America many times as a child and even as an adult. It was the closest thing to Disneyland that Northern California had to offer. I'd ridden the rollercoasters, eaten the food, played the games. I wondered now if my feet had walked the same paths Beverly must have walked day after day for...how long? Her rides in the Sky Whirl would have been years before my own journey. Did she leave an imprint? I wondered. Could her energy or essence or whatever metaphysical dust Lily might explain have lingered...or touched my soul even then?

"How long did you work there?" I asked.

"Oh," she said, still lost in a kind of reverie, "just the summer... my dad...well, that was Labor Day weekend. Everything changed after that."

She snapped back to today, and all I could think to say was, "I'm sorry."

She told me it was okay and that it helped to know I understood what it was like to lose a parent, two parents. One lost when we were too young to understand, and one when we knew too much.

I put my arm around her then, held her close, and she leaned into my shoulder as we flew over the city.

"What did you look like in those days? Braces and pigtails?"

"In my twenties? Oh, Perry, I'm not sure you've quite grasped the concept of aging. That's the curse of the young. If you could see the whole picture, you'd understand the whole process. How it lingers... how it slips away."

"The days are long, but the years are short? My mother used to say that," I offered.

"And it's true. But there's more to it than that. It's like, again and again, we're called on to make the most important decisions of our lives when we're least equipped to make them. I mean, how to choose a college major when you know so little about what needs to be done in the world? And how can you commit your life to marrying one person when you've only experienced twenty or even thirty years' worth of people? How can you rebel when you're not old enough to understand the cost of mutiny?"

"Life forces us to make choices, for sure," I said softly. "But, nothing's forever. We can always change our minds, point ourselves in a different direction."

"Somethings deserve forever," she whispered.

We sat there in silence for the last few minutes of our ride, and just as we came to rest again on the loading platform, Beverly sat up slowly and said, "Perry, I'm not feeling that great. I think the day has caught up with me. I think I need to be home."

I called Ben even before we got out of the gondola, and he was there in less than five minutes. He'd been nearby all along. Ben anticipated Beverly's needs better than I did. For that, I was somehow both jealous and thankful.

We said our goodbyes quickly and left Lien and Samay to find their own ways home. Lily was attentive and kind in the limo while I sat next to Lucian, cursing my own selfishness for keeping her out so long. Why had I even invited her to something so taxing? Why hadn't I insisted she go home after the concert? Why did everything about Beverly —— about Beverly and I —— seem so right and so wrong, so blessed and so cursed?

Back at Beverly's grand home, Alicia took control.

"I told her this would be too much four days after treatment," was all she said. But her look shamed us all.

Lily told Lucian and me to wait in the library while she helped get

Bev something to eat and into bed. I felt as if I should be doing that. I felt as if I alone should be doing everything Bebe needed. But the truth was Lucian and Lily had been vital parts of Beverly's life for far longer than I, and so I willingly, if hesitantly, stepped back to allow them their connection. They too had this right and privilege, I knew.

"I shouldn't have kept her out so long," I told Lucian as we entered the library—which was literally a dark and leather-furniture room with ceiling-high wooden bookcases on every wall.

He poured us drinks as if we were in some old movie: *Brief Encounter* maybe, or wait, *Now, Voyager*, my mom's favorite.

"She wanted to be there, Perry. And she deserves to get what she wants."

"I guess," I answered, in no way convinced.

"I'm a big believer in no regrets," Lucian said.

"Is that what got you interested in time travel? Fixing regrets?"

"Okay, well, first, it's not time travel. And second. Yes. In a way. But why wouldn't I want to help someone move forward by allowing them to confront and maybe alter their past? After all, isn't that what you do? It's just that you're fixing them in the present moment, allowing them to move forward. I'm doing the same thing, just from another point in their life."

"You believe you can really do that?"

"I've done it, Perry. Not once or twice, dozens and dozens of times."

"But you actually believe you're doing more than just altering memories. You believe you're literally taking them back and changing the past?"

Lucian took a sip of his whisky and sized me up. People have to be worthy of receiving certain kinds of information, and I knew he was gauging me to figure out if I was trustworthy enough to receive the richness of his life's work. Would I hold it dear? Would I carry it tenderly, knowing its worth and fragility?

"Perry," he began slowly, carefully, "I'm sure this is a lot. I know it's difficult to put aside the rigid confines and solid structure of science. But haven't you yourself come up against that ethereal wall? That point where science wanes, and the we-just-don't-know of it all jumps in front of your face and demands you look? Surely you've had recoveries or maybe even deaths that defy reason or explanation? These kinds of things are all around us. They seep into our lives like sand or sometimes flood waters, no matter how hard we try to keep them at bay."

I knew of and even had a patient or two whose cancer seemed to somehow simply disappear. The patients and their families inevitably labeled such things 'miraculous' while we, their physicians, said the treatment had worked. Or *told* ourselves the treatment had worked. Or maybe our diagnosis had been faulty to begin with. It was easiest to say any of those things and tuck the experience away; move on to the next patient.

"I can see it," Lucian said. "I can see in your eyes you know what I'm talking about. Look, don't keep denying it. The most important thing you can do in this life is stay open to the possibility of more. And this is just…more. Maybe *we* are more. Maybe we really *are* eternal souls having a temporary human experience. And maybe part of that experience that we've barely begun to understand is the simple idea that we control our own physical lives and our own eternal energy. That we can direct and focus one hundred percent of our energy. And whenever and wherever one hundred percent of our energy is focused, that is our reality."

I sat with that for a minute. I thought about Mrs. Tollerson, who was eighty years old when we found cancer in her liver. Eighty years old when we explained it had metastasized. A tiny octogenarian who told us she wasn't ready to go and that God would heal her. Mrs. Tollerson told me she had a friend who did Reiki, and she herself had faith in visualization and the power of joy. The same Mrs. Tollerson who came in six months after diagnosis, after having absolutely no surgery or clinical intervention of any kind, and was somehow cancer-free. An initial misdiagnosis or mix-up I rationalized. "You are free to believe that," she told me with a wink. "But I know the truth."

And she wasn't the only one. I couldn't think of many other cases quite as dramatic as the faithful Mrs. Tollerson's, but I'd seen enough to know. Enough to appreciate that we didn't understand everything. What was it Einstein had said? That the difference between past, present, and future was what? Oh yes, *a stubborn illusion*.

"Lucian," I ventured after several minutes, "could I try?"

"What?"

"Would you experiment on me? Would you take me back and help me change a memory?"

CHAPTER THIRTEEN

Here is the part in my narrative where I need to ask you, as a reader—an interested party—to do something. Because, you see, I was going to say that my asking Lucian to include me in his experiments was *that* point. The strange tipping point that changed my life's entire trajectory. But even as I started to write those words, I questioned their truthfulness.

So, instead, I'll ask you to consider those same things I too have examined. Because yes, taking that step with Lucian changed things—but so had inviting Lucian and Lily to the concert. So had leaving the baby shower with Bev and meeting the two of them in the first place. So had my scheming to *coincidentally* drop in on Beverly's infusion, where Lily happened to be. What about the—what was it? Chance? Coincidence?—of Bev presenting a check at the Giants game when I also happened to be there? (Although it was true, I was often there.) But what about me being on call for Ruben the day Beverly fell? What about any of it? All of it?

That's why I ask you again, dear reader, to consider your own life. Your life right this minute, as you read my words. What thousand choices, decisions, and circumstances led you to this moment? Were they all made by you? Did others help force you here? And even if you feel you have absolutely been forced to the exact place in your life where you are right now, how did you contribute to the journey? What choices did *you* make?

For, you see (and you will yet see even more), I have come to believe we are indeed the masters of our own destiny. Yes, I have completely embraced what I once thought of as a kind of fan-fiction theological philosophy. I now believe — have come to learn — that we do, in fact, shape our own time and space and circumstances just as a child pats together a ball of clay. The thing is, as we grow older — and with luck, wiser — it is, I believe, incumbent upon each one of us to gain the patience, the knowledge, and the skill to take that ball of clay and turn it onto a potter's wheel where we can gently shape and mold and add too and take from until we've got something formed by our own hands, crafted by our own creativity, and pleasing to our own minds, hearts, and souls. Yes indeed, I believe we are that powerful.

I heard individually from each of my friends after the concert weekend. Samay caught me first thing Monday morning. Cornered me really.

Not known for his subtlety, Samay barged into my office without so much as a knock and cut right to the chase. "Perry, Perry, Perry… what the hell is going on? What are you doing, dude?"

"Good morning to you too, Samay."

"Look man, I get it. She's great. She's beautiful, or she used to be, or whatever, but this is some serious mother-complex stuff you've got going on."

"Samay. I appreciate your concern, but it's not…"

"Not a mother-complex thing? Grandmother then?"

"Samay!"

"Okay, all right, I get it. But Perry, she's dying, man. Why would you do this to yourself?"

His words gave me that same stomach drop I'd felt on the Ferris wheel's descent. Dying? Even though I understood Beverly's prognosis intellectually, no one had said that exact word. Ever. And, in fact, I'd never truly stared it in the face. But here it was, being flung before me with what felt like a vicious ferocity. Dying? Beverly was sick, but all of my patients were sick, and the majority of them—maybe the vast majority of them…maybe…got better.

"She's not dying, Samay! She's not. She's fighting. She's getting better!"

"Okay, okay, whatever you say. So then, what's the plan? She gets better, and you…what? Get married? Start a family? Grow old together? C'mon Perry. In any scenario—and I mean *any scenario*—this has no place to go. It's a dead end no matter how you look at it."

"Great. Appreciate all your support. Good to know my best friend has my back."

I was instantly furious. Partly because it really did feel like a betrayal. Partly because there was so much truth in Samay's words. The rage I felt toward Samay, yes, but also toward life and fate and timing and cancer, couldn't be stopped. I seldom raised my voice, but now it lifted from my chest to my throat and into the indifferent world.

"But this is *my* life," I told him as my pitch and volume rose. "*My* decision. And I'm going to keep seeing Bev, and that's all I know right now. That's all I have to know right now. And that's all you need to know right now. Stay my friend or don't, but that's the way it is. This is the way I'm living my life, Samay."

I could see Samay, my very best friend, was taken aback by my words and my intensity. I set my jaw, and my gaze didn't falter. He took a breath. His rigid and determined body, his entire demeanor, softened.

He met my eyes, then shook his head and spoke softly, "Perry. Fine. I mean, you're right. It's your life. It's just that I've seen you go through a lot, you know? I don't want to see you hurting again."

I softened too. "Samay. Look, just be my friend, alright? Life is full of hurt. No one can avoid it. Just let me be, you know, happy. Happy in the moment. This moment. Right now."

"And you're happy? This is making you happy?"

"It is."

"Okay then. Okay…"

We were silent for a long time — something that didn't often happen between us. I knew nothing Samay could have said would have moved me off the road that led to Beverly, but I didn't want this. I didn't want other things, other people, in my life to change. No one in the world knew me better than Samay and Victoire and Lien. It hadn't occurred to me that it might be possible to lose them. And even though Samay had just assured me that wasn't happening, I wanted to move back. I wanted it to be just another day between us.

"Hey, speaking of uh, older women, I saw you and Lien leaving together…"

"Older? Are you kidding me? You know I don't date older women! Besides, Lien's not older. She's not…right?"

"She's got practically a decade on you, dude."

"Nah! Really? Are you serious? But she looks so…"

"Young? Beautiful? Smart? Accomplished? Funny?"

"Yeah. All those things."

"Holy cow! I believe the amazing Dr. Shankar might be smitten."

"Smitten? Really? God, Perry, that old lady talk is rubbing off on you. You wanna go have some barley soup and catch one of those moving picture shows? I hear they talk now."

"Jesus Samay, she's like, sixty, not a hundred and sixty."

And yeah, we went on like that for a while. Back and forth. It felt good to joke about all of it because it meant it was real and accepted and that Samay truly was my friend. He had my back, after all.

Lien caught up with me later that same day, and Victoire called me Wednesday night. They had much the same take: concern over what they saw as a repeating pattern in my life—trying to right a wrong that they felt would only lead to a doubling down on my pain. I understood what they were saying, of course, but I didn't—couldn't—explain to them the feelings and connection and security and happiness that I didn't fully understand myself.

I started going to Beverly's house every night after work. Checking up on her health, of course—she was tired, yet happily resilient—but also just spending time with her, talking, laughing, sharing—all of those things you do as a new couple. It was Beverly who suggested I take a good, critical look at why I wanted to get involved with Lucian's memory research. Did I, she said I should ask myself, want to expunge or change the memory of my mother's last day in an attempt to assure myself our relationship—Bebe's and mine—wasn't exactly what my friends suspected it was? And if I were able to appease or even eliminate the guilt and pain associated with my mother's passing, would it change my feelings toward her? As in, would I no longer need to try to save her if I reconciled my failed attempt to save someone just like her?

But that was the thing—the thing I understood at my core—that no one else seemed to fully grasp. Clearly, even Beverly had her doubts despite feeling the same inexplicable cluster of emotions I felt. Yet,

I knew. I knew what I felt for Bev was far beyond any other kind of caring or love I'd ever felt. I could try to use a thousand words that made me uncomfortable. Words like soulmate or twin-soul. It wasn't their supposed truth that made me recoil. It was that they were too small, too ridiculously inadequate, and even supercilious to describe our relationship. They were joke words to skeptics and only the smallest portion of a huge certainty to those who believed.

The most frustrating part of our entire relationship was my own inability to articulate or even fully understand my own feelings. There was no reasoning behind them, no explanation. They simply…were. This was my truth. And nothing could change it.

I stayed each night at Bev's house until she was asleep. Sometimes I spent a long time just watching her haloed shadow in the semi-light before heading home. The night she asked me about my reasons for getting involved in Lucian's memory therapy, I sat in her room for a long time, holding her hand as she dreamed.

In the darkness, with the soft sound of her steady breaths falling down all around me, I wondered if she truly feared healing — my own, not hers. Actually feared that I might not need her if I were somehow able to resolve the pain and guilt and grief that had lain so heavy on my chest for so many years. It hurt me to think she might doubt me, doubt us, but I understood. That is, I understood why people thought what they thought. My trauma, plus Beverly's age and condition combined with my age and history, would — to almost anyone — equal Oedipus or something near to him, a cousin maybe.

But no.

I knew myself, and I knew Beverly. I somehow knew her bigger and wider and more deeply than anyone I'd ever known in my life. And in some way that push into love was also pulling me toward

Lucian and his experiments. And if it were possible...if his methods actually worked, the change wouldn't only be in me. It would be in Beverly, too, and in everyone around us. They'd know for certain that we were more than the living embodiment of a chapter in a basic psychology textbook. Divested of their surety in my psychological hang-ups, how could they doubt? I wanted no one to doubt the truth of Bebe and me, so I was all in. No matter the risks. No matter the outcome.

I say risks because Lucian had already said the same word to me many times. Before we could even try his special therapy, he wanted my medical records as well as a series of other new tests. The biggest worry was an adverse reaction to the phenobarbital or some latent issue with any of my organs, including lungs, heart, and other major players, but not excluding virtually every minor part of my body. This wasn't a game or a lark, he insisted again and again.

When he was satisfied I was a healthy enough specimen to take part, we began working on details. What did I remember about the day in question? Music? Smells? Other sounds? Anything that I associated with the day.

I told him about getting the call on the last day of my OB-GYN rotation and being surrounded by the other students. The look the attending shot me when my phone vibrated in my pocket, but Lucian said we needed to go back further. Not a lot further of course, but if we went back to that specific memory, I still wouldn't make it to my mother in time. So, what else did I remember from that day? Or the day before?

This was something I hadn't thought about in a while. Or maybe forever. What did I remember from that day?

Back in those days, if you had asked either of us if we were living together, Victoire and I would have said then—and I suspect would repeat forever—that we were not. Yes, we spent virtually every hour—both waking and sleeping—together, but my keeping a bedroom in an apartment I shared with Samay and Lamar Pallas made our relationship less-than. Our committed lack of commitment seemed to me perfect since both of us balked (I thought) at the idea of marriage. We were young and still very much on the verge of emerging careers. Our work and school hours were long, and while our relationship was supportive and sometimes passionate, I didn't think we were on a pathway to forever.

Come to find out—and as Victoire later (and then often) said—she was under the impression that was exactly the road we were on. (She said I would have known too if I'd only asked…or listened). When Vic eventually understood otherwise, she ended things very quickly. Michael emerged six months later, and the rest is—painful for me, happy for her—history.

When I started really trying to remember other details of that day, I was reminded of how desperately Vic had tried to get me to forget Dr. Hildebrand and that last day of rotation. My mother was far more important, and everyone would just have to understand, she declared quite emphatically.

We woke that morning as we had for a month or more to an alarm I'd set to blare Arcade Fire's *Wake Up*. It was my little joke because of the song's title, which had nothing at all to do with getting up in the morning, and because, at the time, Arcade Fire was Vic's favorite band. We'd seen them at the Civic the fall before, and I'll be damned if she didn't still wear her t-shirt from the show to bed almost every night.

Victoire was always up first. She'd light her jasmine candle. "It produces beta waves," said she, a doctor, in all seriousness. After her stretches and a short meditation, she'd put the coffee on, which was my cue to hit the shower. That day, she lagged behind as I headed for the door, and I urged her to hurry along.

"I'm riding in with Amanda today," she informed me.

"Why? You don't trust the old G6?" I asked. My aging Pontiac was something of an early-century relic, but it hadn't failed me yet.

"Perry." She got stern now. "You can't seriously be thinking of going in. I'm leaving for the hospital with Amanda. You…you go home."

I looked at her for what seemed like a long time. In truth, I couldn't decide whether to be mad or grateful, and I certainly didn't know what to do. Finally, I opened the door with force and slammed it behind me. In my old familiar car that smelled slightly of the jasmine that always floated around Victoire, I fought a short battle in my head. I should head for the freeway and my mother, I thought, but then I told myself how much she wanted me to be a doctor, how important it was that I finish—that I start saving lives like hers. I'd started off in the direction of the 101 onramp but managed to talk myself out of it and instead turned toward the hospital.

Cowardice. And the single biggest regret of my life.

When I took all this remembered information and spilled it at the feet of Lucian, he was ecstatic. "This is perfect, Perry! Exactly what we need," he said.

"It's enough?"

"Are you kidding? The song, the smell…two smells! The day…do you remember the weather?"

"Cool, foggy in the city. Sunny by the time I got to San Jose."

"Nothing out of the ordinary there, but we can recreate the conditions—at least the cold—that might be helpful. Although, it's all very strong without that."

"So, we're good then?"

"I'm fairly confident you'll see the results you're hoping for."

I'd had very few sick days in my life and rarely went to the doctor myself, so I wasn't surprised when Lucian gave me the medical go-ahead. He said we needed to plan everything for a Saturday so I could go back and then have all of Sunday to recover. Lucian urged me to understand that this kind of cognitive shift could have wide-ranging implications as far as my own mental health. I understood what he was implying—especially for a metaphysical skeptic such as myself—but I wasn't worried. I just kept thinking about the possibility of nightmare-less sleep—or sleep in general.

Beverly, though she loved Lily and respected Lucian—and in fact had initiated the idea of my seeking his help—had become less keen on the idea. I understood. Aside from the issues she'd lightly alluded to concerning our relationship, Bebe personally had also, quite necessarily, developed a firm "what's done is done" attitude that had seen her through some very tough times. She understood the weight of guilt and regret I carried. And yet, she'd ultimately triumphed in virtually all of her many difficult circumstances and felt strongly that our past experiences shaped our future destiny. She wanted healing for me, but it was hard for her to let go of the notion that our lives could or should be any different from what they were, which was an accumulation of all the moments—good and bad—that had brought us to exactly where we now stood.

I didn't disagree exactly, but as someone who'd spent his life trying to heal people—to make their lives better—I was determined to do whatever was required to ease my own pain. It was a heavy load I had carried for a very long time, and while its weight was always encumbering, lately it had gotten to be almost too much to bear. I had to try.

It was three weeks, more or less, until we were able to schedule my memory session. We had hoped for sooner, but during that time, Bev had two chemo sessions, and they had left her weak and frustrated. Her arm seemed to be healing nicely, and in fact, the cast was scheduled to come off before my planned adventure, but even that fairly cheerful news did little to get her thinking positively. I'd seen this phase often in my practice. Chemo and other cancer therapies could be brutal. There inevitably came a point when the perpetual body punishment seemed a fool's errand.

But, for most everyone, a patient's Gethsemane moment gave way to a perseverance that always seemed to me both biblical and miraculous. They continued to ask why they had been forsaken but almost always commended to modern medicine their body and spirit.

I spent hours talking to Bev, not out of duty or effort to buck her up but rather because I cherished our time together, and her fight had become mine. Often, we would pull out old and dusty photograph albums that narrated Bev's life from her very earliest days to her most recent accomplishments. She had dozens of such books. A writer and chronicler of time, indeed. Some of the earliest were in the form of scrapbooks with photos and memorabilia pasted onto thick paper. Notes about her feelings, thoughts, experiences, and more were written in every corner of the pages with a variety of colored pens and in Bev's swirly handwriting. And poems…so many poems. Some of them were silly, others angst-filled and cringe-worthy teenaged screeds. But many, very many, were poignant, insightful, lyrical, and moving. I thought her writing brilliant. The totality of her art, photos, thoughts, and feelings was a kind of startling introduction—or maybe reunion—with the girl she had been. In photos, her blond hair was long, thick, and straight. There was never a time when I wished the Beverly I knew to be anything different than what she was in our fleeting moments together, but I also longed to have known that teenager in cutoff jeans and a 49er t-shirt in front of the big house, washing her first car: a champagne-gold Camaro.

What would we have talked about if I'd known her then? Would she have even liked me, a skinny nerd with a painter's eye? But even those musings were short-lived, and when brought from the corners of my mind into sunlight, seemed patently ridiculous. I understood our relationship with a deep part of me that had no questions. We had known and loved each other always. Time didn't exist, Einstein had said, not in the linear way we understood it in our lifetimes, so in the all-together always, the *expansive present*, as others called it, we simply knew and loved and existed together eternally. I was not a religious man and had, throughout my life, scoffed at metaphysics and those who chose to believe in wished-upon connections to an unseen world. But now, I lived within it. I could no longer deny anything.

"That's how it happens," Lily told me one day when I was at her home preparing my future and my past with Lucian. "One day, you have an experience, and suddenly you see more. You understand more."

"My mind is blooooowwwnnn," I said in my best hippie voice. But Lily was serious.

"Your mind is expanded," she said. "Your heart and your soul are opened."

Sitting on the long, white couch in Beverly's sprawling living room that was lined with shelves surrounding a marble fireplace, I was content in a way I never had been in my life. Here, there was no reason to hide, or fear, or even plan and strive. We simply lived. We held each other. Talked. Laughed. Sometimes, we watched TV.

Sometimes I read to her. Just like Miss Gibbs in sixth grade, remember? We were—to put it in its most basic, human terms—happy.

The weakness she was feeling concerned her greatly. She sensed a decline—again, a normal part of the chemotherapy process—but I assured her the treatment would work and it would all be worth it when she was back to normal—taking on the world once again in a Beverly Bowen whirlwind of strength, wisdom, knowledge, and caring.

She often closed her eyes when I spoke and cajoled and made these kinds of promises and would eventually murmur something like, "Mmm, I hope so," or "If you say so, Perry." I wanted more fire from her and her promise as well. But I settled for her nestling contentedly into my shoulder or with her head resting on my lap. I had enough fire and determination for the both of us, I knew.

CHAPTER FOURTEEN

We began very early on the Saturday of my induction. I had—after much consideration and a great deal of hesitancy—asked Samay to be part of the procedure. He was reluctant and very skeptical, of course. So, I didn't mention Lily's alleged success or any kind of metaphysical or—God forbid—spiritual aspect to the process.

This, I explained, was government-funded research, cutting-edge stuff. Because of my recurring nightmares, PTSD as it were, and one crucial memory that I could attempt to access, I was a perfect candidate for Lucian's study. And who wouldn't want to be a part of an emerging scientific field of research?

Samay was nothing if not a sucker for knowledge. And if learning meant a new discovery and perhaps the fame and glory that went with it—well, that just made it all the sweeter. In a way, that drive was exactly what had led Samay to specialize in anesthesiology. He was determined to understand—or try to; it was quite an inexact science—how our bodies respond to pain and in what ways they are able to block it—with or without modern medical aid. Samay's curiosity had seen him involved in many research studies over the years. And he excelled in his work.

Of course, his work and reputation were aided by the fact that Samay was generally better with people on a short-term basis (just ask anyone he ever dated). So short introductions and explanations followed by extended periods of unconsciousness suited both him and his patients. For the time they knew him, his patients loved Samay.

Bev and I arrived an hour or so prior to when I'd told Samay to be at the colorful house in Berkeley. I wanted to get Beverly settled and chat a bit with Lucian before we began. Lily had the TV room all set up with pillows and blankets on that plush sofa, along with a side table overflowing with water, fruit, veggies, Lily's homemade hummus, and other goodies. Bestla rested nearby in what I'd come to think of as his big, floppy security mode. He was a beast who loved his protector status and, indeed, the one he protected. For her part, Beverly fussed over Bestla that day and every time she saw him.

"Bestla-boy in the world," she said in a high-pitched voice while petting that huge noggin of his.

Lily smiled at the scene and then turned to Lucian and me. "We're going to enjoy some *us* time while you guys do your *you* time," she said.

It was a joke she was telling. As if they were two ladies from a sixties sitcom. It was funny because nothing could be further from the truth. The truth of Lily and Bev was that they were forces to be reckoned with. We — both Lucian and I — would rather have had them by our side during the memory induction, of course, but also everywhere, always. This kind of male-female partnership was new to me. I'd spent years wrapped up in myself, thinking of relationships as less partnering and more accessorizing. But I recognized now what I'd been missing. I saw it in Lily and Lucian, and Victoire and Michael; and the Shankars, Kabir and Hema; and the Royers, Martine and

Bernard; and I imagined between my parents at one time, and the Grand-mére I loved and the Grand-pére I never knew.

I felt it between Beverly and myself. It was a connection that asked nothing because everything was freely given. It was a calm and simple joy in being together, without a plan or a purpose or event built upon the idea of needing to do more. We were enough together. I had grown to understand the depth of Beverly's education, experience, wisdom, and insight. I cherished her sense of humor that was both astute and wickedly sarcastic when the situation called for it. I wanted her by my side constantly because she built on to me. She added height and width to my being, and I wanted this new structure to stand forever.

Lily and Lucian never questioned our relationship. They accepted us as we were and asked nothing except that we treat each other well. This was never said in words, but it was how they lived their lives, and I knew they expected the same from us and from everyone. The world, I knew, let them down constantly, but I would not. Beverly would not.

Walking out to his lab, Lucian asked me to sit for a minute on the rocky half-circle that wound around a small firepit. It was autumn by then, and while this was a time for some of the best and warmest weather in and around San Francisco, the mornings remained—as nearly always—damp and cold. I had on a sweatshirt and jeans but didn't relish spending more time in the morning air than was absolutely necessary.

Still, when Lucian motioned for me toward the stone seating and asked simply, "Sit for a minute?" What could I do? He sat too, and I could see he was wrestling with the idea of whether or not he should divulge something. I worried he was about to call off our morning session and asked him just that.

"No, no, of course not," he assured me. "I wouldn't have had you come all this way, this early, if I were just going to turn you away." He half laughed.

"But you do have something you need to tell me, right?"

"Well, I don't know if *need* is the right word. But, Perry, I could use someone to talk to. Someone to tell."

I didn't like the seriousness of his tone. It was worrying. "But Lily. You could tell Lily…" I was trying to distance myself from words I might not want to hear.

"Lily knows, of course," he assured me. "She might be telling Bebe right now; I'm not sure. Depends on if she seems up to it. We thought we'd play that part by ear."

"Lucian, you're kind of scaring me now," I said slowly.

"I'm sorry. It's not scary. Well, it kind of is, but nothing scary directly related to you…if that makes sense."

"It doesn't, but I'd be really happy if you got to the point where you explain it."

Lucian looked at me, looked at his lab, took a deep breath, and began. "Two days ago, I had a visit from the big guys at StratCom. US StratCom, the government guys I work for. Well, the people who fund all this." He swept his arm to indicate the lab and sighed. "Well, you know. At least, you know some of it. They're intelligence. That is to say, military and spy stuff and all that. I told you they were interested in healing soldiers…"

He tapered off. Lost in his own prior beliefs.

"And…they're not now?" I asked.

"No. I mean, yes. They are. And they've been very supportive and enthusiastic about my work. But about a month ago, they invited me to a video conference with lots of folks on the call. Some doctor there, an M.D., not a Ph.D., was asking questions about integrating memories. Exactly what you'd asked about it. See? You're right there with the military bigwigs."

"Don't forget the spies," I tried to joke.

"And the spies," he acknowledged.

It was true. Not long after that first dinner we'd all shared, and just after I'd talked to Lucian for the first time about trying his process myself, I'd asked him about sharing someone else's memory. I guess the road my thoughts were going down was obvious to Lucian, though I was trying desperately to seem a casual questioner. You know, someone who was just interested in…science.

"You talk to Bebe about this?" he asked immediately.

"No. No. It's just a question. Just wondering out loud."

Nothing was further from the truth, as I'm sure you, dear reader, have already surmised.

The previous night, Bev had been telling me more about her last summer of freedom spent working at Great America. She talked about the friends she'd made, the dances, and employee-only after-hours park openings. I thought of her as she was in a scrapbook picture where she was wearing bright orange knickers and a sailor's top — the standard uniform worn by employees in the turn-of-the-century portion of the park back when it first opened. Her hair was long and pulled back into a high ponytail, and she was laughing — that same deep and open laugh she still had, I imagined.

One of her most prominent memories, she told me, was of the *Carousel Song,* a tune played over the park's loudspeakers at the opening and closing of each business day. Beverly joked about her lousy voice and refused to take part in karaoke even when Lily, Lucian, and I fairly begged her to during one of our many dinners together at their home.

But that night, she was dreamy and caught up in the memory that seemed to swirl around and envelop her like a haze.

"See the carousel," she began singing quietly, "turning round and around there. It's a fantasy, take a ride, and you'll see. It takes us along as it sings you a song. It's a daydream..." She stopped then. Laughed a little and said, "See, I told you I couldn't sing."

But she was wrong, and it was beautiful. I told her as much, but she was a little embarrassed and more than a little teary-eyed.

"I don't know why I'm so maudlin tonight," she said.

"You'd be surprised how much I like maudlin," I told her.

Much later that night, when she was asleep and I was wide awake searching for sleep, I got on the internet and searched for *Great America, Carousel Song*. As always, my phone did not disappoint, and sure enough, an old picture of the Santa Clara Great America Carousel popped up while the song played in the background.

It was a spritely little tune that began with a kind of oom-pah calliope, and I could feel the horses rising up and down with each three-quarters beat. I imagined that girl, cancer-free, with her whole life ahead of her, and my eyes welled just as Bebe's had. I was touched that Bev had shared this memory with me but also brokenhearted. And that's when I first had the thought...the same thought as StratCom apparently.

"So, the call was a month ago, and then they wanted to visit?" I asked.

"That's it. I mean, yes, but they just suddenly showed up. No warning. Two generals and God knows how many of their minions," he said. "All kinds of ranks. I'm not good with those kinds of things, but lots of stars and bars, you know?"

I imagined every military movie I'd ever seen and nodded my head yes.

"They brought equipment too," he said.

"More? That seems almost impossible."

It was a joke, but Lucian didn't laugh.

"You'd think so. But Perry." He drew close now and lowered his voice. Did he think they were listening? "They want me to begin experimenting with cross-memory sharing right away. They want me to devote all my time to it." Now, even quieter and with a kind of panicked desperation. "Perry, they want to be able to tap into prisoners, or I don't know, spies or terrorists, or whomever—tap into their memories and see what they know, what they were told, what they might have done that will tell our guys what they might be thinking of doing!"

"Wow," I said, genuinely at a loss for words for a moment. "And is it possible?"

"I think maybe it is. There are other researchers who have had bits and pieces of success, but Perry, I'll be honest with you. I think my research is far more advanced than anyone else's, and StratCom knows it."

There was anguish on his face, and he literally sat wringing his hands for a moment.

"Perry…Perry, think of the implications! I've been doing this to heal people, and they want to turn it into a weapon! And that might seem swell if it saves American lives, but I can't even begin to think of all the ways it might be used. Petty criminals? Thieves and shoplifters? What about potential suspects? Dissenters of any kind? 'Let's just pop into your memories and see what you've been thinking about!'"

"Good God," I said quietly. "It's Orwellian."

"Yes. Orwell. I thought Vonnegut, but Orwell too. I don't know what to do. I can't be a part of it. I have no desire to be the twenty-first-century Oppenheimer," he sat silent for a protracted couple of minutes. I was quiet too, scrolling through the frightening possibilities in my mind.

"I'm sorry, Perry. I didn't mean to lay this on you, but it's been driving me a little crazy."

"It's fine. I'm glad you said something, and we can definitely postpone or cancel today if you want."

"Cancel? Oh God, no. This is the kind of thing I *want* to do. This session today is going to remind me of why I started my research in the first place."

"You hope," I said, trying to remain guarded in my optimism.

"I *know*," he said.

Samay showed up shortly after our conversation.

We were still sitting outside in the cold, and Samay was quick to point that out. "Is there a reason you guys are out here freezing on stone instead of inside a nice, cozy little lab?"

We both tried to step back into our lives—strange as they happened to be at this moment before trying to alter a memory—but not so strange as what we'd just been discussing.

Samay hadn't seen the lab before and was appropriately awed at the setup. I was fairly shaken myself. Since the last time I had been there, only a few weeks previous, another exam table and all the associated components had been added. If I'd thought the amount of equipment Lucian had in the lab was impressive and crowded, this was almost comically over-the-top.

Sophisticated and expensive machinery was everywhere. Another bank of computers had been added, and I was sure there were more cameras in the room. A second skullcap and accessories sat on the new bed, and everything seemed to pulsate like a 1950s sci-fi movie.

Samay stammered out his shock and admiration, wondered aloud if he could get some kind of government grant to do his own "out of this world" research and "live the good life." Lucian said the government had plenty of money to spend and plenty of warlords who wanted to spend it.

"You sound a bit cynical, Dr. Phanes," Samay said.

Lucian smiled but spoke words that might have been a joke to Samay but rang with a truth I understood. "Frankenstein, Strangelove, Jekyll, Moreau, Phanes; all doctors. What does that say about the possibilities of the profession?"

Samay laughed and said, "Okay, I get it. We'll get started on the movie about your life, right Perry?"

I nodded and tried to get us back on track. We were, after all, there for a reason. "Then we should probably do something movie-worthy or at least book-worthy."

"Right, right." Lucian was back. "To the work at hand, then."

From there, we proceeded as if engaged in some standard medical procedure. I was hooked to monitors, including an EEG that would track and help isolate the location of my memory. The skullcap, with its dozens of sensors, fit snugly and uncomfortably but felt appropriately detailed and scientific. What came next wasn't exactly ordinary, so the cap helped me feel grounded.

After the equipment was attached and I was settled on the exam table that, in truth, was more of a comfortable bed, Lucian began guiding me into a kind of meditation. I followed him through breathing exercises as he tried to have me quietly disconnect from the day, from my normal, always-running thoughts, and my now-life. During this time, he began sensory stimulation. I noticed the smell of jasmine and coffee. Finally, Arcade Fire began singing *Wake Up*.

"It's the last day of your OB-GYN rotation, Perry. Early morning. You're just waking up. Think about it. Remember it…"

I could see it clearly, every bit of it, from the blue flannel sheets to Vic's Arcade Fire t-shirt. Even as I began remembering, I could hear the machinery beeping. I knew Lucian was mapping my memory. I knew he'd found the right spot. It was all so vivid. How could he not?

"Okay now, Perry," Lucian said after some time. "I've asked Samay to go ahead and administer the phenobarbital. You're going to feel very drowsy, but I want you to stay in the memory. You may feel a mild sting…a stimulation from the electrodes. You may not feel it at all. Just remember."

I did. I stayed there and then—even as I heard the music get louder and a few quiet words between Lucian and Samay—the world, the world of my present—began to slip away. And the memory began to solidify and at some point, I realized I was no longer observing the memory. I was in it. What I mean to say is that it was no longer a memory. It was real.

It was real, however, with a difference. Because in this new-past, I was completely aware of my present, why I was there, and what I needed to do. And yet, everything was solid and true and happening as it happened before. But this time, *I* was different.

As I sat in my bed, wearing the clothes I had worn then, looking the way I did then, Victoire again walked in from the kitchen to tell me coffee was ready and again begged me to consider not going into the hospital that morning.

She looked young and lovely and concerned and kind, and how foolish I'd been! What had I lost and given up because my eyes became foggy, my brain muddled, and my soul angry and broken by grief? I pulled her to me and kissed her. Her lips were soft, and her hair smelled like jasmine.

"I miss this," I said.

"You don't have time to miss this." She smiled and kissed me again. "C'mon Perry, just get in your car and drive to San Jose. Forget everything else. Go see your mom."

It was all overwhelming, the immediacy of the moment and the density of the day inflaming all my senses. But I knew. I knew. I knew I was there for a reason, and I knew the consequences that lay ahead if I failed to follow through with my mission.

"You know what?" I asked, then answered, "You're right. To hell with the hospital and school. Let them kick me out of medicine for all I care. I'm going to see my mom."

"Okay, well, Perry, nobody's going to kick you out of anything, but I'm glad you changed your mind. I've got a ride, but you better get up and get going. The sooner you're out the door, the sooner you're with your mom."

I moved quickly then, but I have to tell you it was quite an effort. I was back in time, and it was all real and every little thing I did startled me and touched me and evoked feelings I couldn't name. I shampooed my hair with the Old Spice stuff I'd used all through college. The bottles had changed in my present, and it sent a kind of nostalgia combined with glee to see the old style—though it had been only a few years—packaging.

Getting back into my car was the same. It smelled the same, felt the same, and ran the same way. The freeway traffic hadn't changed, but the car models, even the newest ones still sporting dealer's license plates, were, to me, nearly a half-dozen years old. My car radio was set, as always, to KNBR, and they were talking about the Giants, but it was a season gone by. I knew the outcome. They did not.

It was dizzying, mind-bending, but I tried to put it aside as I once again raced down 101 and screeched into my mother's driveway. But this time, Carmelita wasn't at the door. This time, the door was locked, and I had to knock. When I flew past Carmelita as she opened it in surprise, I ended up breathless at the side of my mother's hospital bed. Winded and sweaty, I inhaled deeply and tried to sound casual and happy.

"How's my best girl?" I asked.

And my mother, my living, breathing mother, opened her eyes, turned her head slightly, and said, "Oh Perry, I'm so happy you're here. I was afraid I was going to miss you."

It was a strange and eerily prescient thing to say, but all that mattered was that she'd seen me. She knew me, and she was happy I was there.

"Mom," I whispered through tears, "of course I'm here. Where else would I be?"

Then I told her I loved her, and she told me she loved me. Those were the last words we said to each other. And they were the right words. The perfect words.

Her breathing changed not long after, but Carmelita didn't have to make an urgent phone call to me. I was there. I held my mother's hand as she passed, lay my head on our joined fingers, and cried when I knew she was gone. I didn't think I was sobbing, but maybe I was because I gasped a little, trying for air. Then, my chest started to hurt. I stood up then, hunched over with both my hands on my mother's bed. I was trying to steady myself and trying to fight off the pain while trying to catch my breath.

Then, like a movie theater going dark before the feature attraction, the room began to swim in blackness, and I could hear the far-off sound of voices. They were coming nearer, and I was lost in darkness and confusion and pain.

CHAPTER FIFTEEN

"What the hell is going on?"

It was Lucian's voice. I recognized it now.

"Get that oxygen on him! Does he have a heart problem? *Did you know he had a heart problem?*"

Lucian was demanding information from Samay that I knew he didn't have. Neither did I. I was fairly cognizant of where I was now and what was happening. Lucian was yelling at me to relax and to breathe, and they were everywhere around me, trying to ensure my safety, my health, and my complete return.

It took a while for me to begin to feel better. My heart arrhythmia subsided, and though still drowsy from the phenol, I began to perk up and take stock of the whole remarkable experience. I could only explain it in the simplest of terms. I didn't yet have the strength and would never possess the vocabulary to truly articulate to Lucian and Samay what had just happened.

While Lucian was making sure I got saline and Samay listened to my chest, I just kept repeating, "I was there, guys. I was really there. It was all real. Every bit of it was real, and I changed it. I did it right this time."

And then there were tears that I couldn't control and couldn't stop, and I thanked Lucian again and again. I don't know what Samay thought, but I didn't care. I knew what had just happened to me, and it seemed miraculous. Lucian had led me to Lourdes, and I'd bathed deeply and been cured. My God. The past, I knew, would no longer haunt me because that haunting past no longer existed. The tears finally eased, and I felt better. My body was tired, and Lucian was more than a little concerned and very flummoxed by what had happened to me, but I was elated. I felt I could have danced across the garden back to the main house. I begged to be let loose from the machinery so I could tell Bev and compare experiences with Lily.

But Lucian was cautious. He wanted me to rest, to be fully restored before I did any kind of celebrating. And he reiterated that there were still many tests he needed to perform.

"This has never happened before, Perry. We need to figure out if it was you or it was me. It's serious."

I was still straining to breathe normally, but I was completely lucid. "C'mon Lucian. You said Lily's first experience was difficult too. Maybe it's just the nature of the beast."

"No, Perry. This was different. Lily's heart never…this is serious, Perry."

"Yes. Serious. I understand. But Lucian, you just saved my life — maybe twice — you should be ecstatic! Shouldn't he be celebrating, Samay?"

I saw the look that flashed between the two of them, but Samay said success should always be celebrated, and after just a while longer, I was up and wide awake and anxious to get to Beverly.

I walked through the backyard ahead of Samay and Lucian and was aware of their concerned murmurs behind me. But I didn't care.

The only thing worth talking about, as far as I was concerned, was the success of the day. To me, the experience was so obviously real that I was ready to slap a "breaking news" post across social and every other type of media. This was an absolute scientific breakthrough. And it wasn't purely scientific. This somehow connected us to our deepest selves. Our souls. After all, if I could literally return to the past and correct errors, didn't that speak to some type of divine universal construction?

I had thought about this a lot prior to that miraculous day of my own. If Lily had gone back and erased her very physical scars, did she then alter history? Or simply create a new one? And why didn't we all do this with our own memories? I'd thought so much about how the day of my mother's passing should have gone. So why didn't it change?

According to Lucian (in a theory that was massively influenced by Lily), it was all dependent upon that very particular issue of focus.

"We are in this moment — this absolute here and now — because this is where we direct our focus," Lily had explained to me. "Our consciousness — our soul, if you will — is, of course, eternal, immortal. And if time is nonexistent in eternal reality, why are we so bound by it in physical existence?"

"Life is physical," I had said simply.

"Exactly!" Lucian and Lily exclaimed in unison, then laughed at their own enthusiasm for what they thought was my understanding. Truthfully, I was more than a little lost, which my face must have shown.

"Look," Lucian began. "We're willing participants in this physical time and space experiment. But the idea is that we don't have to be trapped by it, that, in fact, we aren't! We are focused in this very second — you and I and Lily — *that* is why it is real to us!"

He grabbed Lily's hand and then mine. Lily took my other hand, thus joining us in a circle of human reality.

"I can see, hear, touch, smell you because we separately and jointly agree to focus on this moment in this life, in this space and time. But Perry…there are innumerable other options available to us. Possibilities and probabilities we can explore…or use," Lucian continued.

"So what? We can just time-slip? Like Billy Pilgrim? We're all living in a Vonnegut novel?"

"It's not exactly like that, but the idea isn't that far off. Except for the one definitive lifetime thing."

"Ah, so now we're back to parallel lives?"

"Yes and no. It's more like exploring all options. But if we are focused on this point in time, as we agree we all are now, we aren't aware of the other choices we might make, or perhaps have made…"

"Then who am I really? Perry here now? Perry in some alternate life, who made different choices? When does the real Perry please stand up?"

This was the basis of a kind of existential crisis. Who was I, if not myself? Did Perrys, in other alternate lives (which I didn't actually believe in but which had a very vague feeling of truth…possibly…maybe), have the same questions? Did they even have souls to consider?

I didn't like the idea of conscious beings contemplating the meaning of existence but having no soul to return to. That is, being empty vessels. I had never claimed to know about or even believe in a God or an eternity or any kind of life after death. I'd been casual and aloof about it all, noncommittal to the point of scoffing silently at others' childish beliefs. But now, the idea of not having a soul seemed to collapse onto everything I had begun to understand about myself.

All those things I'd questioned at best or mocked at worst seemed to me now very urgent and real. Who had I been kidding? What had I been avoiding? It was as if I'd spent 30 years planning a great bakery heist only to get caught with my hand in the cookie jar.

What if I'd finally found the treat I so desired, only to be discovered and left with nothing?

Lucian let go of our hands and sat back, looking at me. Lily patted the hand of mine she'd been holding.

Her voice was hushed and understanding. "Perry, they're all you. Your energy. Your soul—if that makes it easier to visualize—dispersed in vast and distinct experiences involving this life as Perry Roberts. It all comes back to you. Your oneself, enlarged and enlightened by this lifetime, these many experiences."

"And what about the idea of past lives? Real or ridiculous?"

"Same opportunity, different circumstances."

"So, you think past lives are a thing? A real thing?"

"What do you think?"

I knew the answer, of course. Not in truth for myself, but I understood their belief systems better. Truly, if I hadn't seen Lucian's lab and known about his government contract, not to mention the respect for his research within the scientific community (yes, I'd done my own research about his research), I would have laughed all this off, dismissed this couple as crazy hippies and gotten Beverly away from them as fast as possible. As it was, I was being forced to contemplate ideas that threatened to send me hurling headlong into some kind of metaphysical meltdown.

I tried my best, for several hours and over the course of many different dinners and visits to their home, to question and maybe even trap Lily and Lucian in a cage of their own ideas. Instead, I had found myself stepping inside only to find it wasn't a cage at all, but rather a doorway, with an open door at that.

"But," I had countered one evening after yet another amazing Lily-made meal, "you are here, Lily. Why didn't your change simply send you onto some other scarless timeline? Or is this it? Are we a part of one of your parallel lives? But if that's true, it's a huge circle of problems. Did Lucian and his research exist in this parallel life? Is it a huge loop? You always got the scar just so it could later be removed? What's reality then? Is there reality? It doesn't make sense."

I felt like the dim student with teachers patiently trying to help me latch on to a concept. Master this concept, the teacher might say, and you can graduate to the next level of understanding.

"It's all real, Perry, that's the point," Lucian explained, with Lily nodding in agreement. "It's just that we're focused on one aspect of our total reality."

They were like a tag team of philosophical understanding. Lily chimed in now.

"You see, that's where Lucian's research comes in. His combination of medication and electrical and sensory stimulation—all exacted over a long time, a very long time, Perry, allow us to unfocus and refocus and unfocus again. I came back to this timeline because I wanted to…because I was aware of it. I wanted to come back, and Lucian's methods helped me do that. That's the difference; we're aware of this lifetime. Even as we venture into the past, we remember this present and the linear path we are on in this lifetime. Throughout my own experience, I remembered my purpose. Awareness and choice, that's the difference. That's why I came back, and that's why I have no scar."

This made sense. I mean, as much sense as this whole uncanny, bizarre set of circumstances could make. "But what if you didn't want to come back? What if you decided to stay with your grandma and relive all that without the scar?"

"But that couldn't happen, Perry," Lucian assured me. "Because I was in medical control. After the allotted time, I would have simply ended the experiment, woken her up."

I accepted it then, and now had experienced it myself. Here I was, unburdened. Free. Who wouldn't be relieved and, in fact, elated to know they'd been with their mother — or father or spouse or sibling or friend — at the time of their passing and that the last words either of you uttered were declarations of love? I was giddy with the freeing of my heart, the lifting of the black cloud that had surrounded me since my mother's death and threatened constantly to smother me altogether. My existence was suddenly bright and sunny and open, and I felt the breathtaking possibility of life without regret.

CHAPTER SIXTEEN

For some reason, I half expected Lucian not to mention the heart issues or whatever it was that happened to me medically during the memory treatment. But I couldn't have been more wrong.

Lily and Bev greeted the three of us with expectant faces as we walked in.

"Well?" Lily instantly asked.

"It was amazing" was about all I could muster.

"So amazing it practically killed him," Lucian added.

They gasped, of course, and asked what happened, and Lucian was more than happy to fill them in with every detail. I knew he wasn't being malicious or even invading my privacy—this was an experience we were sharing, after all. I had done similar things myself, talking diagnoses and treatments through with someone (often Vic or Samay) just to hear it said out loud. Hearing my own words fly into the ether allowed them to come back to me in a new form, and that was sometimes enough to push them to make sense and provide answers.

"Perry insists he's never had heart issues, but are you sure, Perry?" Lucian asked.

Fact was, I wasn't. I'd just never been sick, really, not in a way that would necessitate hospitalization. And I'd easily passed any screenings for school and the self-testing we did as a learning tool in medical school and beyond. My own explanation was that I'd merely been hyper-stimulated by the overwhelming sense of reality coupled with the intense feelings of grief and release. I was fine. And I told them so.

"Not only fine," I told the disbelieving group, "But better than I have been in years…seriously."

"I'm sure you feel that way, but we really should do some further tests. You could have a number of issues," Lucian said. "My first guess would be some type of congenital defect that only surfaced now under these unique conditions."

"That would be my guess as well," Samay chimed in.

"Look, I'll get a checkup. I'll do whatever. But I'm telling you all, I'm fine! I'm fantastic! Let's celebrate!"

The two doctors glanced at each other once again before Samay told Lucian, "I'll make sure he does."

And Lily finally exclaimed, "Well, yes! Let's celebrate! I'll make mimosas, and Perry, get ready to tell us everything! Leave nothing out!"

Lucian kept the mimosas out of my reach, but I was drunk enough as it was. In fact, I couldn't remember when I'd felt such easy elation. I was without guilt or regret: an innocent man.

We spent the entire afternoon talking first about my experience, then comparing mine with Lily's. We speculated more about parallel lives and past lives and time travel, as it were, and the possible implications and uses of such therapy. One thing we hadn't addressed in the lab, but about which we speculated all afternoon, was the question about the passage of time.

Lucian had, of course, carefully recorded start and stop times for my induction. According to him, I had been under exactly 27 minutes when my heart began its unnatural beating. I told them how at both endpoints—when going under and when coming back—I could hear Lucian's voice as if it were coming from somewhere within or around my memory experience—as if my life were suddenly being narrated. And again, just as when I entered the memory, I had total recall of it all.

The biggest difference, however, was the length of the experience. I'd begun my memory as planned, the early morning of my mother's passing. But it had been a long day. I'd talked to Vic in the morning, had a cup of coffee, driven to San Jose (easily forty-five minutes for that alone), and stayed at my mother's bedside. To me, it had been hours—perhaps seven or more, I wasn't sure. But whatever the exact length of my stay in the past, I knew it hadn't been 27 minutes.

Lucian said it had been not as long, but with similar variations in time perception for Lily and others of his research subjects. (Lucian and Lily had each mentioned this when they first told me about her experience, but I hadn't thought much about that aspect of the procedure.) Lucian said he'd spent considerable time trying to figure out if there was a mathematical equation that would, if not explain, at least apply. One hour in memory time for every five minutes on this timeline?

But the only thing he could say for sure was that he couldn't say. One thing he did note was that for Lily and me, who had had the deepest and most physically-felt experiences of anyone, the time spent within the memory was considerably longer—nearly an hour for Lily and several hours for me—as opposed to several minutes or up to a half-hour.

I trusted that Lucian would find the key at some point and, in the future, be even better equipped to allow for these longer stays. He wouldn't let it go until he understood what was happening, of that I was sure.

Throughout our long discussion, I half expected Lucian might open up about the visiting generals he'd hosted and the demands US StratCom was making in regard to his research. But he was tightlipped. It occurred to me then how purposeful Lucian had been in speaking to me outside in the cold, sitting on a damp, rock half-wall. Did he suspect his home was bugged? There were cameras everywhere in his lab, but I'd assumed they were for Lucian's own benefit, for safety's sake, and for record keeping. But did others have access? And if so, were they accessible with Lucian's blessing? Or did the government trust in his innocence? Or in his unstated complicity?

One thing I'd come to definitely understand that morning was the power of Lucian's method. I'm not certain how it could ever be protected against individuals and organizations who would seek to weaponize it, and that made it not only incredibly valuable but also incredibly dangerous.

Throughout my life (and like everyone, I suppose), I'd heard all kinds of people make all kinds of claims about things that were supposed to change the world or that were revolutionary in one way or another. But this.

This.

This thing, this method, this process Lucian had developed was more than just revolutionary. This could do more than change the world. This could fundamentally alter the way human beings understood reality and their place within it. Once it was out, memory repair would affect every aspect of existence. Regret could become an archaic word with no real meaning for future generations. Religion of almost any kind would have to shift and reconnoiter to make their ideologies fit within this new, real, all-encompassing paradigm.

And what if Lucian's brain-to-brain experiments worked? How, then, did human relationships of all kinds change? If I were truly able to understand someone else's experience—very literally walk a mile in their shoes—would our common smug indifference or righteous indignation become a relic of the past?

Could criminals be made to witness and even feel their victims' pain? Could struggling students log on to their teacher's brain? Download understanding? And for all the positive possibilities, there were doubtlessly an equal number of selfish and wicked uses I knew I probably didn't even have the capability of imagining. It might begin with national defense—securing our nation's safety by knowing things kept hidden in the mind of those who might seek to destroy it—but where would it end?

I thought of Vonnegut again, Cat's Cradle and Ice-9: a simple tactical defensive tool that ultimately ended the world. That's what happened when you didn't think things through, when you didn't consider the implications. If it were true that since 1945, we'd nearly universally feared humanity would be lost to a bang, could it also be true that it might instead be lost to a thought? A memory?

Such ideas sent my mind looping around and around, only to hit a brick wall of rejection in the same way it did when I tried to imagine eternity. My life—all our lives—were built upon beginnings and endings. How could we understand anything else? Still, we hoped. Didn't we?

Late that same night, after Bev and I had spent the evening talking—not just about the day, but about our own memories, especially the ones that seemed on the forefront of our lives and that repeated over and over again—I sat at her bedside, waiting for her to fall asleep.

I knew the day had been a lot for her, and although I had wanted Bebe there and she had wanted to be close by, I felt guilty. I knew my own issues and the whole damned and blessed memory repair had overshadowed her far more serious health issues for weeks now. I had been working when she had her cast removed, and although I'd promised to try and be there, I couldn't manage to get away from my own patients and missed everything. Ben had walked her in and driven her home.

I was able to sit with her through at least part of her last two infusions, but it wasn't enough, I knew. Now, seeing the worry and weight of her life relax from her lovely face as she drifted off to sleep, I knew I'd been greedy for her attention while offering little in return. Holding her frail hand, I thought of how our images must have looked from afar. Seeing the scene in silhouette, I imagined a blue light running through her and into me. It was a romantic and mystical impression I would have scoffed at only a few months prior. But now it came to me as a gift. I understood it as our literal and figurative connection and was grateful.

I vowed in a whispered voice (but aloud for the Universe to hear) that from that very moment on, my all-consuming focus would be on her.

"Only you, Beverly Bowen," I promised. "Only you."

I had no intention of creating another regret. I didn't ever want to have to desperately try to fix anything between the two of us.

Beverly and I had not officially named what we shared and offered each other, but after that day and night, I fairly moved into Bev's home, and so yes, we were living together. I spent most of my off-time there anyway, but now I brought more than just a day or a week's worth of clothing along with many books, photos, and knickknacks that were dear to me so that Bebe's spacious home held everything I loved.

We spent our evenings talking, sometimes walking around her well-appointed neighborhood—until that became too much for her. Often, we'd watch old movies—some comedies from her youth (*What's Up Doc?* And *Paper Moon* were favorites; she was a big Bogdanovic fan) and many very old movies that she'd first watched with her own father (*The Best Years of Our Lives*, *The Enchanted Cottage* and anything with Cary Grant we watched again and again.) She told me more than once how she'd read a book called *Up a Road Slowly* as a fifth grader and had vowed then to become a writer herself. It was perhaps her own biggest regret not to have kept writing.

"Why didn't I just write? There was nothing stopping me from coming home and writing at night or when I wasn't working. Why didn't I just do that, Perry?" she asked one night.

"It's not too late. There's no reason you can't pick up a pen or open up your computer right now."

"No." She sighed. "So much is gone, and everything else is buried. I can't reach it. I don't have access anymore."

I tried to assure her she was wrong and encouraged her to at least try, but she'd tell me she was tired, and I knew she was.

One night, she pointed to a book out of her vast library as another I might like to read. I sometimes read to Bev to help her fall asleep and often read silently to help myself with the same thing. When I sat and opened the book's well-worn pages, a piece of paper slid out.

I'd read a lot of Bev's poetry but had never seen this before.

I sat down next to her with the book and the paper with her sweet handwriting and read aloud.

Today, while the blossoms still cling to the vine.
I'll taste your strawberries. I'll drink your sweet wine.
A million tomorrows shall all pass away.
Ere I forget all the joy that was mine today.

"That's beautiful," I said.

"It is!" she chuckled. "But I didn't write it. They're lyrics to a song. You know how I am."

It was true. She had dozens of notebooks filled and half-filled with her own writing but also with phrases she liked. Quotes she'd heard and, most often, song lyrics. Song lyrics were poetry with the natural lilt made manifest, she'd told me once. Bev longed to write songs, but the inner workings of music were lost to her. There were a handful of tunes she could toy with on her grand piano, but the ability to read music had always alluded her, and all her poems, she said, were vain attempts to create songs.

Her vast vinyl record collection was overwhelmingly dominated by singer-songwriters: Carole King, Joni Mitchell, Carly Simon, Bob Dylan. She had multiple copies of everything Paul Simon had ever recorded and a smattering of newer artists she deemed worthy. We often listened to her collection, and she was happiest when music was the background of her life.

But I didn't know this one.

"Oh," she said. "We haven't listened to John Denver much. I guess we should."

What I knew about John Denver could be condensed into one Rocky Mountain High, which seemed a bit hokey and not terribly special, but Bev insisted that Denver's best stuff was his lesser-known songs.

"His version is actually a cover, but it's the best as far as I'm concerned. I listened to it over and over again all one summer—the summer I was at Great America, as a matter of fact. I had it on eight-track in my car!" She laughed.

Bev had me find it among her collection, and as we listened, she sang along. Her voice was tender and misty. She'd long ago lost her inhibition when it came to singing in front of me. She may have been unsure of her vocal ability, but how she loved to sing. Bev no longer had the strength of voice to belt out her favorite 70s tunes from CCR or the like, but this song was sweet and gentle.

> *I can't be contented with yesterday's glory*
> *I can't live on promises winter to spring*
> *Today is my moment, now is my story*
> *I'll laugh and I'll cry and I'll sing…*

Her voice trailed off as John Denver repeated the chorus of *Today*, and when the song ended, she had tears in her eyes. I wiped them away with my thumb and kissed her wet cheeks, then her sweet lips, and held her close while she cried and I hid my own tears.

CHAPTER SEVENTEEN

I'd always taken for granted that phone calls coming in the middle of the night or ungodly hours of the early morning were inevitably bad news. But as with all rules, there are, it seems, exceptions. Of course, I've also been told that exceptions prove the rule, which I came to find out was also true.

About a week after my memory shift, my phone went off at five in the morning. We were nearing winter now, and the days were short, and that morning, at that time, very dark. It was Samay, and I immediately feared the worst. Him? His parents? Someone else we knew? It was bad for sure.

"Vic wants us at the hospital," he said without any other kind of introduction.

My heart sank and then began to beat wildly.

"Oh my God, what happened?" I asked, the panic rising.

Samay assumed his clinical voice, "Well, Perry, it's like this…about nine months ago, Victoire suddenly and inexplicably found herself pregnant. And now, wouldn't you know it, that baby insists on being born…she's having the baby, man!"

I could breathe again.

"Oh! Oh, of course! I'll be right there!"

I'd woken Beverly, of course, and invited her to come along, also of course, but she said I should be with my friends. She needed her sleep. I agreed that she needed to rest and told her I'd see her later at the hospital anyway, as she was slated for another of her regularly scheduled infusions. I threw on some clothes and was out the door.

The roads from Bev's house to the medical center were relatively quiet, but it was still an hour from phone call to parking lot, and by the time I got there, then up to labor and delivery, Samay was waiting for me.

"Five-twenty-three a.m., dude. Dominique Martine Hines. Eight pounds, seven ounces. Twenty-two inches long. Mother and baby doing fine. Father is a wreck."

"Oh wow! That's fantastic. Grand-mére is going to be so thrilled. Mrs. Royer too. Have you seen her? Seen the baby?."

"Nah. I feel like it's their time right now. I mean, I'm here, and you're here, so the pact is intact, but you know, we should wait until after the family has their chance."

I sometimes forgot that things had grown and shifted and changed so much between the three of us. Michael and Victoire and now baby Dominique were the family. I had nothing to do with them. Except, of course, that I would always feel somehow connected to Vic and her parents, Martine and Bernard, as well as Grand-mére, Dominique by name. Still, I was the outsider now. Casually tangential to the whole but far outside the middle. I no longer had any claim of belonging.

This wasn't something I fretted about or even thought about that often anymore, not with Bev in my life especially, but sometimes even things far distant can feel like a loss when you're once again forced to meet them head-on. But I was also honestly happy for Victoire and Michael, relieved that both mother and daughter were safe and healthy, and eager to see them all.

Somehow, I had pictured, or maybe hoped, that I would see Victoire and baby Dominique alone. But, of course, when we finally were invited into her room, it was already filled with people: Michael and Vic's loved ones. Victoire's parents were there along with Michael's and Grand-mére. Vic's brother Andre had come up from L.A., and Michael's sister, who I didn't know, was there as well. We greeted everyone and marveled over the tiny new human who had an inordinate amount of hair for someone only three hours old. It was, in a way, surreal, and I couldn't help thinking about could-have-beens.

But it was a joyful morning, and truly wonderful to see Vic so happy. Tired but happy. I hugged Victoire and whispered congratulations, telling her little Dominique was beautiful, just like her mother.

"Thank you," she whispered back, then asked, "How is your friend?"

This was the terminology people around me had come to use in regard to Beverly. No one would utter any label like "girlfriend" or "partner." Everyone, it seemed, with the exceptions of Lily and Lucian—and, of course, me—kept our relationship at a distance by not giving it a name. I didn't pretend it was anything but what it was, which is to say, a relationship between two people very much in love, but others left things where they felt it was appropriate. They could only acknowledge us with blinders on.

It hurt, but it also didn't matter at all. Samay seemed to have softened quite a bit. Especially since he'd been witness to the resolution of my past and not long after asked me, "Mother issues resolved, and your feelings for Beverly haven't shifted? Haven't changed even a little bit? It's okay to admit it, you know? Even she would understand."

"Samay," I told him then, and it hadn't changed since. "Bev is the first person I wanted to tell about the experience. She's the first person I want to tell about all my experiences every day. And she will always be."

"Sounds like love, bro..."

I smiled to have him acknowledge that. It meant a lot to me.

"It is," I said.

Things hadn't progressed that far with Victoire. She didn't know, of course, about Lucian's treatment and was still very "concerned" about the context *of* and reason *for* my relationship with Bev. But any explanation or further discussion of the subject on that day—Dominique's birthday—wasn't right, and I answered her question with a simple "good" and then went to shake Michael's hand and hug Grand-mére.

We give old people, especially kind and wise old people like Grand-mére, a lot of leeway when it comes to what is and isn't appropriate to say or talk about in any given situation. Such had always been the case with Grand-mére, and it didn't change that celebratory day.

After I hugged her, Grand-mére took my hand, nodded toward Victoire and the baby, and whispered, "Look, *cheri*, you see? This is a future. You must find a future, *cheri*."

In my mind, I thought, "I will. I'm trying. I am." But those thoughts were filled with images of Bev. I only smiled but had no words for Grand-mére. I wanted to tell her, tell everyone of the love that filled my heart and my life. I wanted to talk about the future. I longed to be able to plan next month or next year or any combination of tomorrows, but there was nothing beyond that day. And I worshipped at the altar of each new dawn that included Bev in it. I praised the sun when it set upon her living, breathing face and sang silent hymns to the moon when it cast shadows across her sleeping frame each night. Suddenly, I wanted very badly to be away from this family photo that included today and a million tomorrows, and I excused myself with another lie about preparing for early appointments.

Just as I was leaving, Lien arrived and squealed with delight when she spotted the baby. She headed there first, and I saw Samay move next to her and place his hand on her back. She looked from the baby to him and smiled.

Had I been so caught up in my own world of medical experiments and medical treatments that I'd missed this? Clearly the day we'd all spent together at Mr. Shankar's concert had blossomed into… something…and I'd been oblivious. And so, it seemed Samay's acceptance of my relationship with Bev might have had some other impetus besides my unchanging affection. After all, if Lien was nearly ten years older than Samay—and I knew her to be—then maybe his understanding had grown on multiple levels—including one obviously very personal. I liked this. And now I had a reason to smile once again.

I'd taken pictures of the baby with my phone, and that gave me even more reason to want to see Beverly when she came in for her chemo just after lunchtime. I was making my way to the infusion clinic when I got a text from Bev.

On your way down? It asked

Yep, I texted back. *Almost there.*

Come to Ruben's office instead. Came the reply.

I suspected she wanted me to walk her to the clinic. She was not always steady on her feet anymore, and I decided I'd grab a wheelchair and insist she ride to the infusion center instead. There was one outside the door of Ruben's office, so I figured we were set.

When Bev said Ruben's office, I expected to find her in one of the exam rooms—pre-infusion work of some kind, not at all unusual.

But instead, she was sitting in his regular office. She in an orange fabric chair, he behind his desk.

"Ah, Perry. Come in. Come in," Ruben said when he saw me.

"Come sit by me," Bev added, patting the other orange chair beside her own.

If you've made it this far in my memoire, dear reader, you have already seen the ways in which, to this point, I had changed. Now, I won't say that over the few months I had known Lily, her bohemian and metaphysical ways had rubbed off on me completely, but I will tell you that in that moment and upon walking into that room, I felt a change in the air — a shift in the energy, as she might say.

I sat down cautiously and had no idea why I was feeling so… afraid. This was, in fact, the first time I'd met with Bev and Reuben since the day he'd invited me to her appointment after the accident. Even then, we hadn't discussed her medical history. Everything I knew about her condition, I'd learned from Beverly herself. Yes, clinically, I'd wanted to know more. To be informed of every decision and a part of her medical team, so to speak. But Bev was adamant about keeping any suggestion of Dr.-patient out of our relationship. I could infer a lot because of my specialty and experience with cancers such as hers, but in truth, I knew, basically, what Beverly wanted me to know. And that day, she wanted me to know something.

Beverly took my hand as Ruben began to speak.

"I'm not sure how many of the details you know, Perry, but obviously, you're aware of Beverly's ongoing treatment. She has, in fact, been going through similar treatments off and on for…what? Two years now?" he asked Bev.

"Just over," she said.

"You're aware also, I'm sure, that Beverly's cancer has metastasized, and treatment is meant as a way to prolong life, not a cure."

Beverly squeezed my hand and looked at me expectantly. I nodded numbly. Here I was, quite suddenly, sitting with all my nebulous thoughts and fears made solid and thrust in front of me. Did I know this? Maybe. But had I allowed myself to think about it? Realize it? Definitely not.

My throat felt full, and I had difficulty swallowing. I'm glad I wasn't asked a question or to contribute in any way to the conversation because my voice was caught behind a wall of tears, and releasing either would have melted me into an inconsolable puddle on the linoleum of Ruben's office. I forced myself to swallow hard and with difficulty.

"Perry, I…" Beverly began but then couldn't finish and looked to Ruben for words.

"Perry, Beverly has decided to discontinue her chemotherapy."

I turned to her frantically, eyes wide, but still no words.

"The side effects have gotten worse, and I don't want these days… my last days, Perry, to be spent like this."

"Last days? Last days, Bev…what are you talking about? You look good. You've been eating better…you said you gained two pounds!"

"We're not saying Beverly has a matter of days, Perry. But there is an inevitable conclusion to this condition. Whether we're talking weeks or months, we don't know. You, of all people, understand how fickle cancer can be…"

"This is what I want, Perry," Bev managed to say.

I nodded but couldn't quite comprehend what had just happened… what was happening. Months? Weeks? I hadn't let myself consider any of it. There was just today and then another today, and Bev was tired, or Bev was doing better, or Bev had an infusion or an appointment, and then there was another today. I hadn't allowed myself to put a timeline or a deadline to anything, and now that they — Ruben and Beverly herself — were forcing me to, I felt the future beating me savagely. This was a fight for which I was unprepared. I was stunned by the blows but managed to keep hold of Bev's soft and impossibly thin hand and walk with her to where Ben and the car were waiting. I hugged her and then helped her inside, watched the car drive away, and all the while, Grand-mére's words were playing in my mind, "Look, *cheri*, you see? This is a future…"

CHAPTER EIGHTEEN

I didn't want to go home that night—home to Bev's, that is. I was confused and sad, yes, but more than anything, I was angry. It was odd to feel the emotion of anger but not have a destination for it, a target at which to aim it. I wasn't mad at Beverly. How could I be? She'd spent years fighting a battle lost before it began, and it had taken its toll. She was the only one who could make this decision, and because I knew her so well, I also knew she had looked at this from every angle, from everyone's perspective, and pronounced a verdict she felt to be right, knew to be just.

My belief in a God of any kind reads like a novel to me. There were times when I'd begun to feel totally immersed, baptized in every word, but even with what seemed to be many truths, in the end, I felt the weight of fiction. Thus, it was difficult to direct my anger at a deity who was elusive if real, ludicrous if fiction, and who may or may not have cursed us both. Maybe I should have ranted and raved about big tobacco and its destructive, heartless agenda, or maybe Daniel E. Bowen for pushing his sweet, artistic daughter into a pressure-filled world of power and position.

But in the end, there was no one. No *one* thing and no *one* person to blame, and that made me even angrier.

I sat at my desk for an hour or more after I'd seen my final patient that day. My mind filled and emptied again and again, and still, I had no clear vision or idea of what to do. When my cell phone rang about seven, I assumed it was Beverly and almost let it ring and ring until the sound faded into oblivion. But she might have needed something. There might have been a problem, a new complication. So, I drew the phone from my lab coat pocket.

I was surprised to see it wasn't Bev calling at all. It was Lily. I hesitated only because speaking to anyone who knew Beverly might forge the truth into a steel I couldn't break down, but again…what if something had happened?

"Perry, I was afraid you weren't going to answer."

"I thought about it."

"She said she told you. Are you okay?"

"Did you know about this?" I felt that anger rising to my throat.

"That she made the decision? No. That she was thinking about it? Yes."

I was furious at the thought of Beverly and Lily talking about the rest of her life, the rest of our lives, without me. How could they? I felt hurt and betrayed, but as I began to respond, to rail at my exclusion, I was surprised to hear my own voice crack and feel the tears begin to fall. It wasn't anger after all. It was simply sadness with nowhere to go.

"Oh, Lily," I managed to get out, "how could she…how can I…"

And then my words were lost to sobs. These were the same kinds of tears I cried the first time I lost my mother, but there was no redemption to be had now, in this moment—this real and happening-now moment.

Lily let me go on for a while before she tried to speak again. Then she was gentle.

"Perry…Perry…listen…I know you love Beverly. I know she loves you, and I know you'd do anything to help her…"

"Yes…yes…anything."

"Then do this for her, Perry. Allow her to leave on her own terms."

"Leave? Leave? How can she be leaving, Lily?"

It was a silly, desperate thing to ask. Beverly and I had only known each other for a matter of months. Only loved each other for those few long and beautiful weeks, and even as we grew closer, she'd always been leaving.

"Perry, Perry, listen. I've asked Beverly to come stay with us. She's already been in touch with hospice…"

"Hospice…" I echoed, shocked by the mention of the word.

"Yes, hospice, and I just feel like she should be someplace a little cozier and more comfortable. And I know you want to be there for her, but you can't be with her all the time—not when you have to work and all. But you're welcome—we want you to—stay here also. Of course."

"What does Bebe want?"

"She likes the idea, but only if you're okay with it. You're her second priority, Perry."

"Second?" I asked out of reflex, not jealousy.

"She's first, Perry. She has to think of herself first. I know we're all here for her, but this is her journey to make, and none of us can do that for her."

When I was a kid, my mom used to take me to Santa Cruz. It was an inexpensive day-long adventure that we both loved. I was cautious in the saltwater, having been dunked by random waves many times.

So I spent much of those days standing on the shoreline. I'd allow the remnants of foamy waves to rush around my knees and ankles, then teeter as the water pulled away and carried with it much of the sand beneath my feet.

I'd spend so much time in those depths that on the car ride home and long into the night, I could still feel the push and pull of the unrelenting ocean against my legs.

Now, I stood teetering on shifting sands once again. I would do my best to remain upright — for Beverly's sake — but I felt myself being pulled into a sea of dark and treacherous depth.

. . .

A few days later, we moved Beverly over to Lily and Lucian's home. They had their second bedroom set up with space for everything she needed, including a new TV and a big, soft chair meant for reading but also for me. They had only two bedrooms, but I was welcome to their couch, they said, or, of course, the bed if we chose.

I hadn't noticed a lot of change in Bev when she decided to end her chemotherapy, but now that I was anxiously watching, signs of decline were everywhere. She had little appetite and was clearly losing weight. I remembered the same in my mom, understanding then, as now, that the cancer was using all the nutrients she managed to keep down to feed its ravenous self. Along with her growing weakness came a sometimes loss of balance that grew worse each day. She had trouble sleeping but had morphine available on demand as both her pain and insomnia worsened.

Bev let Ben and Alicia go with hefty severance packages, and both had come to see her since. They were more family than employees. Neither of them knew it yet, but they were featured prominently in her will, as were I, Lily, Lucian, and a host of charities and other friends and employees. I had balked at knowing anything about her will or, in fact, even discussing such a thing, but she told me she needed me, and well…she needed me.

I kept working, though I managed to get help from colleagues and reduced the time I spent at the Center. So, my days were made up almost entirely of Beverly, who I couldn't let go, and my other cancer patients, who often left me — and sometimes broke me — though I shed no tears.

One night, about a week after Bev had moved in with the Phanes, and after we'd watched some comedy during which Beverly and Lily made continual comments about the ways they thought it could have been funnier (And they were right. They both had wicked senses of humor.) I decided to head back to my place on Mare Island — where I hadn't been for weeks — when Lucian pulled me aside.

"Can we talk?" he asked.

"Sure," I said.

"In your car?"

"Uh, sure."

By this time, Beverly was fast asleep — the result of an exhausting day and morphine — and Lily was doing something in her craft room.

We walked out to my car without saying a thing.

"Maybe drive around a little," he said.

I was freaking out a bit, not because I didn't know what was going on, but because I thought I did.

"I know I must seem paranoid," Lucian said after we'd driven a few miles. "It's just that they…came back. Colonel Riley and his minions. And they're pushing me, Perry. They want more testing, more data, more everything. And they want it yesterday."

Colonel Riley wasn't the biggest wig at StratCom, but he was the number two guy in the Intelligence Division there. He'd been with the original assemblage of military leaders who'd first broached Lucian with their nefarious plan. Now, it seemed, he was in charge of the project and pushing Lucian hard to get busy executing their comic book machinations.

"I can't do it, of course," Lucian said decisively.

I looked at him but said nothing. He was, in effect, having a conversation with himself, and I was just along for the ride, literally.

"It's crazy to think I might hold the key to some kind of authoritarian, dystopian, or Orwellian future. But I think that's what it comes down to. I think that's the truth of it."

Lucian looked down so his face was in shadow, but I could feel his anguish. And I agreed with his assessment as well as his worries.

"I have a plan. Or a kind of a plan…I actually thought of burning down the lab, trying to make it look like an accident, but our house, the neighborhood, you know, I couldn't take the chance."

He fell silent again, and I thought it was probably time I said something.

"Why not just hold them off? Keep up with the research you want to do and just keep failing at the other? How are they to know you're not trying? I mean, the reality is it could take years, decades even to achieve something like that, right? Just keep failing, and pretty soon, they'll take it off your plate. Give it to somebody else, which is bad, but at least it's not you. And you're so far ahead of anyone else it could take…who knows how long before they get anywhere near true thought or memory transference. Meanwhile, you get to keep helping people like me."

"But Perry." Lucian looked up again, and a strip of light reflected from streetlamps fell across his eyes. "I've tried it. And the truth is, I think I can do what they want right now."

CHAPTER NINETEEN

I got home late that night but couldn't wait until morning to confront him. The phone rang and rang, but I didn't care if he was asleep. I didn't care if I woke him from the greatest dream of his life. If my call went straight to voicemail, I didn't care. I vowed I'd keep calling until we talked. But I should have known he'd pick up. In our profession, we always picked up.

"What's going on?"

Always the response to calls at this time of night. A hello meant wasted seconds.

"Why didn't you tell me about the experiment?"

"Ah, Perry. So, he told you."

"We're supposed to be friends, Samay. And I'm the one who introduced the two of you. Why would you keep it a secret?"

"It wasn't a secret Perry. Well, maybe from the guys with the guns and the stars. It's just that you've been preoccupied for weeks. And we understood that. We didn't want you to be taken away from… where you wanted to be."

"I want to know everything."

"Didn't Lucian tell you?"

"He gave me the bird's eye view, but I want to hear it from the bird."

"Okay, okay," Samay said. "But Perry, it's two in the morning. Can we meet tomorrow? I'll tell you everything. Every last detail. But I gotta sleep, man."

I knew waiting until morning would likely mean a sleepless night for me, but I needed Samay alert and articulate, so I reluctantly agreed.

"My office, tomorrow, as early as you can arrange it."

"Sure. Sure. Tomorrow. I'll be there."

"Good."

I hung up without a goodbye. My brain couldn't indulge in any kind of niceties or polite customs. Brain-to-brain transfer and three of my best friends involved in it! I believed Samay when he said they hadn't meant to hide it from me. But I was an integral part of all this, and the fact Lily and Samay had gone someplace I desperately wanted to go brought back memories of the time I'd urged him and Victoire to go away on spring break, as we'd all planned, while I stayed home to watch over my mother when she first started chemo. I was where I wanted to be, needed to be, and I'd insisted they leave after all, but it hurt to know they'd gone on without me.

The fact that everything now revolved around memory while history seemed to be repeating itself was another kind of bitter irony I was ready to escape. And I promised myself I would.

Here is what I found out when Samay came to my office around noon the next day:

Samay had invited Lucian to lunch a couple of days after my experience. He said he'd wanted to talk to Lucian about me. He was worried, he said, about the heart episode I'd had during my memory treatment. That still worried them both, he told me. Seemed like I was the only one who wasn't worried. But I knew myself, and I felt fine.

The two got talking about the research in general, and Lucian ended up spilling the beans about what StratCom wanted. And Samay said he was immediately fascinated by the possibilities of brain-to-brain transference. Obviously, Lucian was as well, but I never could have guessed the three of them—Lily included now—would set up a trio of experiments attempting to allow Samay to share one of Lily's memories, then Lily to try to share one of Samay's. The final try—Lily as the sharer again—was the one with which they'd finally found success.

"I get it now," Samay said. "I understand how the experience you had seemed so real—or was real. I don't know. I'm still trying to wrap my mind around that question. I didn't just see Lily's high school graduation. I was there. I was there, Perry!"

He said he watched her graduate from some distance, from the audience, as it were. But he'd spoken to other people, and they saw and had spoken to him as well.

I told him it was crazy risky to try something like that with only Lucian in attendance, but he insisted there was minimal risk. In fact, they'd exacted the success with only the mildest of sedatives—over-the-counter diphenhydramine—and a long yoga-like self-hypnosis session. Samay had been meditating since he was a child—one of the few of his father's practices he actually enjoyed—and he said it was easy to slip into an, as he put it, "altered state." Lily too was a seasoned meditator, so they'd believed that heavier drugs might not be necessary. Turns out they were right.

The stage had been set with the smell of California Laurels that had surrounded the high school football stadium where Lily's graduation was held. The music was *Pomp and Circumstance*, of course.

The entire experience didn't last long—maybe twenty minutes in the memory and only half that in Lucian's lab.

"You want to know the weirdest thing, though? I knew what was going on. Lily was easy to spot too, and anyway, they announced her name when she walked across the stage. But when I waved to her and when I ran up to her after the ceremony, she had no idea who I was. She was just…living her life…and I was just there, in it."

This was something new. It was also new that Lily initially thought the experiment had been another near miss. She had no memory of seeing Samay—or some strange guy running up to her claiming to know her—at her high school graduation. She described it as simply remembering but very vividly. She had no sense that she was her now-self revisiting a memory. She said it was pleasant but hadn't felt at all like the visit that removed her scar.

Still, Samay was able to give numerous details about the day—things she hadn't told him beforehand and, in fact, some things—like a beachball bouncing around in the crowd as the principal read her name and the caps being tossed into the air with *Freebird* playing in the background. Some of the details she only remembered after Samay had reminded her of them following the session.

So, what had happened?

Samay said he and Lucian had been over and over it, and the only thing that made even the smallest shred of sense was what I'd thought immediately—and said to Samay that afternoon.

"Parallel timeline?"

Samay looked at me with wide eyes.

"You believe in all that?" he asked.

"I don't know," I said. "But what other explanation is there?"

Needless to say, I couldn't let go of any of the thoughts that surrounded all this. I, like Samay and maybe Lucian, tried to think of any other explanation. But how do you even begin to explain something impossible?

That same night, I handed Lucian a note under the table as the four of us sat at dinner. It was laughably like some B-movie scene, but I believed in so much more than I had only a few months ago, so it was not much of a leap to believe the government—the people who were pressuring Lucian to change the course of modern warfare—had ears everywhere. The note said simply, "Can we drive around later?" but I knew Lucian would understand.

All of my anger at having been left in the dark about the brain-to-brain experimentation had been washed away after talking to Samay. The fact of the matter, one I was facing—we were all facing—in every minute of every day was that Beverly was fading. She was weaker now, less inclined to move unnecessarily or contemplate the future at all. She was barely eating, and I knew it wouldn't be that much longer before she wouldn't come to the table at all. Or try to eat at all. Or do much of anything at all.

I was calm and reassuring at her side, but inside I was frantic. Losing my mother had left a void in my heart, but losing Beverly would mean losing my whole heart, and I didn't know if I would survive it. Everything about Bev seemed to move in slow motion in those days, although she remained as bright and engaged and funny as ever. But her body was betraying her, crumbling around her. We watched a lot of comedy and talked a lot about our individual pasts and the short time we had had together.

That night, the night I'd asked Lucian to take a ride, I took Beverly to bed and was sitting next to her, holding her hand and talking about everything and nothing, when she asked me to go into her dresser to retrieve one of the dozen or so books she'd brought to Lily's. Bebe asked me to shuffle through its pages for a single sheet of paper. I began fanning through and found a bit of stationary, bordered by a floral design and yellowed with age.

"Read it," she said.

It was a poem. A love poem of sorts. It was written in tiny cursive, and it read:

> Pain is a separation; a moving away from;
> An afar
> A never having known, but always having seen.
>
> Hold me close.
> There is peace in hold me close;
> joy and love in the ability to find you.
> Find it,
> in my personal space.
>
> Pain is your absence. Having once known;
> having dreamed so completely builds walls,
> walls that once abandoned
> leave a continually recoiling
> echo.
>
> That means hollow.
> That means empty.
> That means separate.
> That means pain.
>
> Pain is separation.
> But all separation — even in a darkness that drips and echoes

> *and won't end*
> *in time shrinks and condenses and*
> *falls in on itself.*
> *Dies.*
> *Eventually proven temporary after all.*

"You wrote this? When?" The sound of my voice was unfamiliar, and it cracked as I spoke.

"College, I think, or around that time. I found it a while ago."

I found my eyes welling, as they seemed to often those days. We sat in silence for another moment or two before Bev finally said, "Perry, that was decades ago. How did I know to write a poem about you?"

Beverly, induced into sleep by morphine and fatigue, said nothing else that night. After a while, I went downstairs, where Lucian was waiting. I gathered my keys, and we headed wordlessly through the front door and to my car. We drove for quite a few miles before I turned onto the freeway and, for some reason, headed toward the City.

"Going somewhere special?" Lucian finally asked.

"No. I don't know. Maybe the ballpark."

"Season's long over by now, isn't it?"

"Yeah," I said. "But sometimes, I just like to walk around the cove or sit and look at the bay."

It was the truth, and it felt like the right thing to do now. The evening air was chilly and damp, but there was no fog, and the skyline looking toward the Bay Bridge was brilliant. A few people wandered around McCovey Cove — locals with dogs or spouses or special others mostly. A handful of tourists. Homeless regulars. We leaned against the railing, water on one side, ballpark to my left.

"You're upset, Perry, I know. I'm sorry I didn't say anything…anything earlier."

"I'm not upset, Lucian. I was. But I'm not now. I talked to Samay. Honestly, I still think it was unnecessarily risky, but it's the results… that's the thing. That's the thing, Lucian!"

"I know. I know. And I'm not sure what to do with any of it. God knows I can't go to Colonel Riley or any of his…ilk. But how can I continue hiding the advances I've made?"

"Are you sure they don't already know?"

"If there's one thing I know about the government, it's that it's a study in contrasts," Perry said. "On the one hand, they knew about me and my research. They're on the lookout for cutting-edge technology and open to even the strangest theories."

"Clearly," I said and managed to chuckle.

"On the other hand, they can be like bumbling Keystone Cops. They had three different contractors working to put my lab together in the beginning. And none of them seemed to be aware of the others. It was ridiculously inefficient. Then, when we finally got things set up, I assumed they'd have some expert keeping watch over me, but no. They wanted quarterly reports with data, video, and test results. That was it. I mean, Perry, I'm generally trustworthy, but how did they know that? That's why I've been so worried about surveillance, but honestly, I don't think it's really occurred to them. They asked me to buy the video cameras online and set them up myself, for God's sake! 'Send us the invoice,' Riley said! Still, here we are, meeting outside in the dark like characters in a goddamned John le Carré novel!"

I laughed again. This time, it was longer, louder. Then Lucian joined me.

"It's just absurd, all of it!" I said when we regained our composure.

"It is, yes. But it's also real. And I'm no hero, Perry, but I can't let them have this. It's the most fantastic, unbelievable thing I've ever done, and I have to bury it."

"Look, Lucian," I began. I'd been planning this. I knew what I wanted to say. "I'm nothing if not a planner, a strategizer. It's what got me through med school. We can figure this out, I promise. But before it's all over, or before it goes underground or whatever has to happen, I'm hoping you'll help me, just like I want to help you."

"Help you, Perry? I thought you were better. I thought everything had worked out just the way you wanted."

"When it comes to the past, yes. You helped me settle everything in a way I didn't think possible, and I can't begin to tell you how grateful I am. But when it comes to the present and to the future, it's … different."

"I know, and I'm so sorry. Lil and I are both heartbroken, and we're honored to be able to help Bebe…and you…during all this."

I needed to approach the rest of this carefully. I knew how it might come across, and in my mind, I had tried to find exactly the right words to express what I wanted…needed.

"And we're both so thankful for all that you've done and all that you're doing. But, Lucian, I had this kind of idea. You know, the experience with my mother was so real, well, it *was* real! And it's with me now. Every second of every minute of every day. It's just stayed with me. It's inside me and in front of my face all the time."

"And that's a good thing, right?"

"Yes! Oh, yes. Definitely. And you see, when you told me about Samay and Lily, and then Samay told me how real it was for him, well, I couldn't help thinking about how much an experience like that could mean to me…and Beverly."

Lucian eyed me closely — as closely as he could in the dark under vague and distant streetlights.

"Wait. You're suggesting I hook the two of you up and send you into one of Bev's memories?"

"Yes!" I exclaimed, probably a little too excitedly. "And I know the perfect one! You see, she had this last great summer before her father died, and she had to join his business, and it was at Great America, and we've talked about it a million times…"

"Perry, Perry, slow down."

I took a breath. It had all come rushing out. I'd been thinking and planning nearly nonstop, and I was sure I sounded like a madman, but Lucian was patient and kind.

"I'm sorry," I apologized. "It's just…I've never known healthy Beverly…"

"Of course. I understand. Have you talked to Bebe about this?"

"No. No. Not yet. I thought I should talk to you first."

"Okay, well, I understand. Really, I do. But a couple of things. First, you'd have to have Bebe on board, and I'm just not sure that's going to happen. You know how she feels about this — all of this."

"I know how she felt before, but after my experience and…how things are now, I mean, I think maybe she's changed."

"You think, or you know?"

"I think I know?"

I smiled, but Lucian remained serious and focused.

"The other thing is Bebe herself — her physical self. Quite honestly, Perry, at this point, I just don't think she's up to it physically."

"But with the meditation and lighter medication…or maybe, maybe no medication! I mean, it's worth a try!"

"I know it's worth a try to you, Perry, but I'm not sure about Bev.

Listen, you talk to her. I'm not sure you'll get the answer you want, but you talk to her. Then, if she's up for it, maybe we can try. But it's a very big maybe."

"A maybe is better than what I have now, Lucian. I'll take a maybe."

CHAPTER TWENTY

I wonder if I've been able to explain to you the true nature of Beverly. It wasn't just that she was beautiful and thoughtful and kind and funny and intelligent—though I know together all those things seem quite impressive. But I think what I may not have been able to adequately express is the way those things came together in whatever situation or circumstance she was in.

To have her tell it, you'd think it was the most natural thing in the world to give up your own dreams to fulfill a father's last wish. Or just an everyday occurrence to take over the helm of a multinational corporation and not only keep it afloat but expand and strengthen it. And how many truly wealthy people have you ever met who actually treated employees like friends or family?

One of Bev's great sorrows was that she never married and never had children. But she moved past her disappointment to support a number of children's and women's organizations, and I'd personally seen her speak to complete strangers in the hospital and offer comfort, support, and yes, often money—though they would never know it came from her.

Beverly loved the beach, and we spent long hours there before she'd become too weak to walk on the sand—or make the drive. She loved trees too, and one of our first official dates had been down to the redwoods. Bev had dogs and cats over the years, but said after her last pup—a golden retriever named Waldo—crossed over the rainbow bridge nearly ten years before I met her, she'd decided her life and lifestyle were too busy to adequately care for another dog, who would inevitably end up spending more time with the help than with her.

"I loved all my pets, Waldo especially. He was such a good boy… for fourteen years!" she told me. "But it wasn't fair to him."

I was suspicious of anyone who didn't love dogs, so it touched me to see her stop to pet and talk baby talk to any pooch she ever came across, and of course, she helped support several animal rescue organizations. That was Bev, involved in anything that might help—pets, people, trees, coastlines, everything mattered to her.

That included me, of course. Despite all she was going through, Beverly always found time to listen to me, all of my complaints, and all of my thoughts, both petty and profound. Even in the very beginning, when we asked the question, had we met before? Did we know each other somehow? What was happening between us, we'd never fully been able to answer. Still, she never made me feel like a fool for developing the wildest theories or questioning the reality of anything…of everything.

It was for all these reasons, for all of Beverly, that I longed for that chance—that last chance—to be with her in a space and time that was free from all that worked against us in our present reality. And, perhaps selfishly, I also wanted to know: would it happen again? Would we connect in the same way?

Beverly moved through life, meeting every challenge with courage and grace. She faced existence where and how it stood, working her way through any problem like sand falling around rocks in a jar. She filled in crevices and found spaces where she could, despite all odds, simply make room. But I tended to question everything. It's what made me a good doctor but a dubious friend and unworthy partner. I honestly appreciated every moment I had with Beverly. She was the greatest comfort I'd ever felt, and brought into my life the brightest joy I'd ever known. Yet, I couldn't help but ask why?

To say that we were an unlikely pair was an understatement. We were less *All That Heaven Allows* and more *Harold and Maude*—both movie references I wouldn't have known before I met Bev. It sometimes felt like a betrayal to ask over and over again—as I did—what is happening? Why Bev? What drew me to her? Or her to me, for that matter? She was so much more than I deserved.

And maybe that was the answer. Maybe I didn't deserve her. Or maybe the intensity of what I felt—what we felt—was too much to sustain. So God, or the Universe, or maybe the Devil, and ugly fate limited the time we could have together. A blessing or a curse or both. Who knew?

I can see now, looking back over what I've just written, that I don't have the words or the literary skill to do justice to Beverly or to what I felt for her during those days or even now. There are sometimes emotions that swell and swirl and bring us to highs and lows and laughter and tears, and it will only ever do to simply live in them, express them. There is no retelling of certain feelings.

Bebe told me once that what we were experiencing was the *still point*. It was after another dinner with Lily and Lucian, another heady discussion of many things. She brought it up because we'd all spent some time talking yoga, what it was and what it wasn't (though Lily seemed to think it somehow embraced all things). Apparently, *still point* was a yoga term, or yoga experience. But Bev knew it from years before; from her college days.

"T.S. Eliot. You know him of course," she'd said. No condescension. Simple statement.

"I know Cats. Do I need or should I say *want* to know more?" I was being fecitious. But this, to Bebe, was not a facetious topic.

"You do, indeed. Or you *should* anyway. He wrote about the *still point*."

And Beverly quoted, as she often did, from pure memory, absolute love:

> At the still point of the turning world. Neither flesh nor fleshless;
> Neither from nor towards; at the still point, there the dance is,
> But neither arrest nor movement. And do not call it fixity,
> Where past and future are gathered. Neither movement from nor towards,
> Neither ascent nor decline. Except for the point, the still point,
> There would be no dance, and there is only the dance.

"We're at the still point, Perry. We're dancing."

And I believed her. I could see us embracing and swaying to the timeless rhythm or our own private song while the world waltzed by.

So, I hope you can understand now, my friends, how much the chance — this brain-to-brain chance — meant to me. And how carefully I considered my words and exactly how I might approach Beverly with the idea. She was declining rapidly, in part, I believed, because she had given way to the idea of leaving. I didn't want to add any stress or emotional pain to her life, but I also couldn't let the thought nor the opportunity leave with her. It was a long shot, to be sure. But it was the only shot I had, and I was determined to take it.

Two days after Lucian and I talked, I asked Bev to take a drive to the beach with me.

"We don't have to get out of the car," I said. "We can just sit and watch the waves."

She was tired, of course, but I knew the beach would call to her, and she agreed, saying she really did "need to see it one last time." My heart sank at her words but was also buoyed with the hope of my plan.

I didn't want to just head to the bay. I wanted the real ocean, wild and open. So, I drove through the city to Ocean Beach, where I knew we could park close to the water, smell the salt air, and watch the waves. It was a longer drive than I probably should have taken, but we brought food and drinks and sang along to a 70s playlist, and time, as always with Bev, passed very quickly.

The afternoon was warm enough (with a blanket draped across Bev's legs) to roll down the windows and slightly recline the seats in my car so we could just…sit. Watch. All the while, I was trying to form the words I wanted to say, and finally, after a half-hour that seemed stalled and stolen, I spoke.

"You knew about Lily and Samay?"

Bev turned her head to look at me, examine my face to find my thoughts.

"I do now. Lily told me all about it yesterday. She was surprised you hadn't said anything."

"Well, to be fair, I only found out a couple of days ago. Pretty big secret they all kept."

"Yes. Secrets."

God, this woman could see right through me. I felt she knew every word I was going to say, but she let me say them. She let me put the words into the air and feel them hover and swallow us both.

"You know it happened without phenobarbital. Just some meditation or slight hypnosis or whatever and a little over-the-counter stuff."

"So I heard."

"Beverly." I took her hand. "Bev. You know how I feel. You know I love you more than I thought it was possible to love someone."

"Yes, Perry. I know. I love you too. At the very least, I hope you know that by now."

"I do. I do Bev. Bebe. But time — our time together — it's slipping away, out of our hands."

"I'm sorry. I'm so sorry, my love."

"But what if we could well, if not make it longer, at least maybe… enrich it? What if we tried to link — like Samay and Lily? What if we went back to your Great America summer? That first day. Remember when you told me about your first time opening? The Carousel song and all that? The summer when you listened to John Denver and sang about a million tomorrows?

"Oh, Perry, I…"

I wouldn't let her speak. I had to keep talking so she couldn't say no.

"Listen. Listen, Bev. I found it on the internet. It's the carousel song!"

I pulled up the song on my phone as I spoke and played it over the speakers in my car. I knew I was sounding desperate, and I was suddenly aware of tears streaming down my face. I hadn't meant to cry. I didn't want to cry.

"I just want to be there with you. With you healthy and looking forward to the future and…"

I couldn't find any words to force out of my throat. They were all caught and useless.

"Oh, Perry," she said, putting her hand on my face, wiping my tears and pulling me toward her. "Can't you understand how that feels to me? I want more time with you—with everyone—too, but trying to experience the past only to have to come crashing back into the present…to reality? It feels…needlessly cruel. And I know you love me, but somehow you wanting to find that 20-something me feels like a something of a…betrayal…"

"Oh no, Bev, no…" I protested.

"I know you don't mean it that way. But all my life, I've had to live up to expectations. My father's, the men in my business, the memory of my mother, the world… But with you, I…I, Beverly Bowen, was just… enough. Can't I still be just enough, Perry?"

I hadn't considered it sufficiently. Once again, I was thinking about myself. My needs. I imagined how the whole trip into the past would be perfect for us both. I had never even considered how it might hurt her. And now, just in the asking, I'd caused unintended damage, and I ached to take it all back.

"Of course. Of course! Bev, you're perfect the way you are. You're enough. You're more than enough! I'm the one who's lacking. I'm the one who doesn't deserve you—or any of this!"

"It's all right, Perry. I understand. It's forgotten, okay? Let's just… sit. Enjoy the waves and the sea."

And so, we did. We sat holding hands for a very long time. Long after the tide had pulled away from the shore.

CHAPTER TWENTY-ONE

Samay caught me again at work a couple of days later. He'd been trying to get hold of me all morning, he said. Didn't I ever look at my phone? He wanted to know. I'd been in a particularly brutal treatment consultation, a younger man with little hope of cure, so I naturally hadn't even looked at my phone, although I'd felt it vibrating several times in my pocket before I slipped it into a desk drawer.

It wasn't like me to do such a thing—emergencies being what they were and Bev being where she was these days—but I'd flipped it over to glance at who was calling just before putting it out of my sight. Seeing it was Samay—and not Lily or the ER or some other person who might be the bearer of distressing news that needed my immediate attention—I figured it could wait.

Who knew how many times the phone rang while stolen away in the dark recesses of my well-ordered desk? I opened it after my consultation to see 15 missed calls and my heart beat suddenly faster.

"What's wrong? Is it Beverly?"

"No. No. Sorry. Bev's fine…as far as I know. It's not an emergency at all, just…urgent."

Turns out, the first five or so calls had been from Lucian. In frustration, he'd called Samay and asked if the three of us could get together for lunch somewhere or maybe drinks after work. I always wanted to get back to Bev as early as possible, so chose option one, and Samay said he'd tell Lucian to meet us at our sandwich spot outside the ballpark around one.

It was ten in the morning then, and I was already exhausted. Those days seemed to me long and thick. I trudged through them as if knee-deep in molasses. Every step I took was an effort, and these meetings and consultations, once just another part of a difficult job, now weighed on me like a cartoon anvil and seemed unending. I didn't know how to consider this changed future. I had escaped guilt and unending self-flagellation once but now seemed fated as Sisyphus, each day pushing uphill a heavy boulder labeled "cancer" only to have it come crashing down every evening, waiting for me to bear its burden again with each new dawn.

This ponderous new reality felt brutally unsustainable, and I wondered how I would endure. Yet, how could I wish for an end? Ending my current misery meant entering into an abyss of torture that was unknown in both depth and duration.

Perhaps obviously, distractions were both necessary and welcomed. So I was happy to walk down to Oracle Park with Samay that afternoon. There was a strong breeze, and the bay air temporarily revived me and lightened me, as it always did. Samay had no real idea why Lucian had asked to meet, so he didn't say much and walked quickly, with determination, moving toward something we knew — and perhaps feared — was important.

I spotted Lucian first. He was dressed in jeans and a black hoodie drawn up around his head. He was in line to order food and looked like a teenager, a criminal, or maybe just a sinner. As we drew up to him, Lucian asked us what we wanted to eat and then asked us to grab a table. He'd get the food. When Lucian finally sat down with our sandwiches and sodas, he got right to the point.

"I've got three weeks."

"Three weeks for what?" I asked, still thinking somehow this was about Bev.

"Three weeks to figure out what I'm going to say in my report."

"StratCom report?" Samay asked.

"Yes. They want something, and I cannot—I *will* not—give them the videos of you and Lily or anything like them. I'm not doing that."

Lucian dropped his head and was silent for a long minute. Samay and I looked at each other but said nothing. Lucian needed time, just as I had at the beach with Bebe, to find the words, to explain himself. Finally, he shook his head, then raised it to explain to us both.

"I mean…I *honestly* thought my work, my research, was going to help people, soldiers in particular. That's why I was so happy to get their funding, the government funding, the equipment, and what I thought was autonomy. I believed them! Jesus, what a fool I've been."

"You're not a fool, Lucian," I said. "The furthest thing from it. And look at all you've done! Look at what you did for me! And I know you've helped so many others. I've seen the videos…that's proof!"

"And that's the problem," he said wearily. "They have their proof of the memory treatment; now they want evidence that I'm making progress on my brain-to-brain research. They want to know how their latest weapon is coming along. They're waiting for me to wake up that sleeping giant again."

"And they're filled with a terrible resolve," Samay added, finishing the quote that could not have been more apt or more terrifying.

Yet, nothing in Lucian's demeanor seemed to admit defeat. In fact, everything he was telling us seemed only a precursor to the real reason he'd called us together. There was, in fact, a plan.

"I've got to get out of this," Lucian said. "Once and for all and forever. But I really could use your help. You two are the only ones I can turn to."

He explained his ideas to us over the next forty-five minutes or so. There were details, of course, but the gist of it was a plot to offer as a report at least two, but perhaps as many as three or four staged videos wherein the brain-to-brain method would fail spectacularly. He'd already been busy duplicating data and then erasing or changing the originals. He was a victim plotting his escape from what was rapidly becoming a hostage situation.

The overall scheme was to frustrate his overlords to such an extent that they would throw their grant dollars toward someone else, some other individual or organization, or even university. His five-year grant period was shortly coming to a close anyway, and he shuddered at the idea of it being extended.

With flawed data and what would seem like very little hope of weaponizing the possibility of brain-to-brain memory sharing, StratCom would move on. At least, that was the hope.

"Look, I know what's going on in the field, and guys, not to blow my own horn and all, but I'm years ahead of anyone else," Lucian whispered, although there was no one near enough to hear. "And that's in large part because of the direction Lily pointed me. Nobody else has a Lily."

He smiled at the mention of her name.

"I'm far ahead of everyone else as far as memory reconstruction," he said. "No one is really even on the same path. And as for brain-to-brain memory transference — memory spying, really — I'm more than years ahead. It's decades, maybe. I might not be able to stop the Big Brother Express. But I can sure as hell slow this train down."

Our part? Lucian needed a safe, off-site place to store his research data and authentic video evidence. That's where Samay—or, more precisely, Samay's dad's property—came in. We'd laughed the day of the concert about Mr. Shankar's preoccupation with safety. He'd hired more rent-a-cops for the day than would have been necessary for an event ten times its size. That got Samay jokingly relating other tales of his security-obsessed father.

He'd shared how years before while touring the property the Shankars now called home, Kabir had been thrilled to learn the land included a 1950s, Cuban Missile Crisis-era bomb shelter submerged in the backyard.

"The real estate agent was trying to explain how much it might cost to remove it. She didn't know that to Kabir Shankar, it was the house's greatest selling feature!" Samay had told us, and we'd all laughed.

Mr. Shankar had gone so far as to refurbish it and further secure it with modern alarm and lock systems, including more than one safe. It was perfect for this moment, this plan, and it seemed almost like fate that it existed at all. For our greater part, Lucian was asking us to become real Guinea pigs for fake brain-to-brain experiments.

"I went to theater camp the summer I was ten," Samay informed us. "I think it's finally going to pay off."

We didn't exactly laugh, but Samay's joke broke some of the tension. We had to move quickly and backdate the videos and data so that Lucian could submit his report of constant failure in only a few weeks' time. He would admit frustration while presenting a report that danced around defeat and bated a hook with the idea that perhaps he wasn't up to the task.

As a conclusive *coup de grace*, he planned to compare his work unfavorably to the "brilliant" research being done by a team of scientists in a private Massachusetts lab—a group he felt was on the wrong path and particularly far away from any real breakthroughs.

When Lucian finally sat back in his chair and slapped his hands on his thighs, Samay and I looked at each other. I again felt that weird B-movie sensation when we said simultaneously, "I'm in."

Over the next three weeks, we worked like mad filmmakers fashioning what we hoped were reasonable facsimiles of failure. There were lots of jokes between us about our abilities to fake fiasco so well, but we felt pretty strongly about our skills feigning disappointment and promoting the idea of a lost cause. It was all a work of good intentions, and big, vague concepts like freedom and justice weighed heavily on all our minds. Even as we planned, set up, and executed our video reproductions of experimentation gone awry, Lucian was spending hours setting up a timeline that made sense for the point at which his experiments began to fail.

He'd previously been so proud and eager to share success. Now, he reasoned it would be most realistic if it appeared he was trying to downplay his "failures." That is, in order to garner the highest probability the government would buy into the idea that his research had hit a brick wall, he wanted to play the "opposite game" that we'd all played as kids: say the reverse of everything that was the truth.

So, my own experiment—which he had yet to report to StratCom—we restaged as an utter failure. With that failure noted, Lucian produced several notes of theories about what had gone wrong. In an effort to boost my memory, we staged a fake brain-to-brain experiment using Samay as my best friend, who had allegedly been present at my mother's death. Here was where we introduced the actual issues with my heart. Lucian edited in footage from my actual memory regression, and I must say, the end result was quite convincing.

Along with that, we staged another destructive brain-to-brain transfer experiment between Samay and Lien.

Yes, Lien. In a relationship I never in a million years would have expected, the two kept seeing each other, and their mutual affection continued to blossom and strengthen. It was amazing to see, as it changed them both in ways I never considered either needed. But then, that's what the best relationships do, right? We brought Lien into our confidence and supposed she—another physician and psychiatrist at that—would lend an added appendage of authenticity to the many-legged octopus we were creating.

Not one of us felt we were breaching any kind of ethical standard. On the contrary, we saw ourselves as something like heroes stopping those with few ethics and great power—a malevolent and possibly catastrophic combination.

Lucian had little time for any real experimentation during those few weeks, and I tried to put the thought of my own memory-sharing ideas out of my mind. But it seemed each day there was some new indication of Beverly's decline, and with each small thing (needing a walker and then a wheelchair, saying many foods, even favorites, were too hard to chew, falling asleep in the middle of a conversation and the morphine; more and more…the morphine), the possibility of a moment without any decay would flash like a bolt of lightning—a bolt of possibility—through my brain.

I ached to be able to take away some of Beverly's pain. Of course, people always say they'd give anything to be able to bear the brunt of a loved one's discomfort or even agony, but I'd never felt the truth of that sentiment in such an all-encompassing, visceral way.

Samay, Lucian, and I began to meet regularly for lunch. I'd reduced my hours as much as possible but still spent mornings at the Center. Samay picked me up in the morning, and we'd all meet for lunch—about the only time Lucian left the house—around noon. Then, when Samay returned to work, Lucian and I would ride home in my car. We hoped we were being paranoid, but there was a lot of discussion during those drives home, and we both felt better having Lucian use my car for our daily rendezvous.

At times, I felt the whole plan a ridiculous folly, but Lucian had been dealing with the feds and StratCom for more than five years, and he said everything he'd experienced led him to believe the bureaucracy, coupled with the number of disparate pies in which the government had its fingers, meant one hand didn't necessarily know what others were doing—and those who did know often weren't equipped to count fingers.

So, we all plowed ahead, trying to believe our own government was as inept as Dr. Strangelove knew. And all the while, even while treating my patients, trying to help Lucian, and loving my ailing Beverly so desperately, the stubborn oom-pah of a calliope slipped into my thoughts, and I heard it like a siren song again and again: "See the carousel turning round and around there? It's a fantasy. Take a ride, and you'll see…"

I felt myself ticketless, discouraged at every turn and by everyone from stepping aboard, but I couldn't let the colored ponies pass me by. I couldn't say goodbye.

At odd moments during the day and for long, sleepless hours at night, I imagined a world of 40 years prior where I saw that young woman, moving through her amusement park life without a dream—or nightmare—of losing her father, taking on his business, giving up writing, developing cancer, finding me.

I knew I shouldn't let it occupy my thoughts, and I knew Beverly—who meant more to me than any fantasy—was hurt by the very idea, and yet, I couldn't let it go. I couldn't let her go.

CHAPTER TWENTY-TWO

They came unannounced. Early afternoon on a Friday. I was working only four days a week at that point and generally no longer than three or four hours a day. Bev was lying on the couch when there was a loud knock at the door, and Bestla, roused from her reverie on the floor in front of Bev, barked furiously and lumbered toward the door. Lucian, Lily, and I assumed it was the hospice nurse who visited daily now. But no. Three men in uniform. One gray-templed, many-striped, authoritative standing in between two young men, close-cropped hair, serious.

"Colonel Riley! I didn't expect you," Lucian said loudly when he opened the door.

I pulled the dog away and heard the man in the middle speaking.

"I didn't expect to have to be here, Phanes," the Colonel countered.

"Well, come in, come in. You know my wife, Lily. And these are our friends, Dr. Roberts and Beverly Bowen."

"Mrs. Phanes, good to see you again. And yes, I recognize Dr. Roberts from your…" he cleared his throat, "unfortunate attempts."

The Colonel looked at Beverly, pale and thin, asleep on the couch. I was sure he understood much from just assessing the scene. Anybody would.

"I'd appreciate having a word with you in private, if that's possible," he said to Lucian.

"Yes. Of course. Shall we head out to the lab?"

"By all means."

The four men headed through the kitchen and out the back door toward the lab. I had a sudden panicky feeling I should be there offering some kind of protection or at least support to Lucian, but I stayed behind, uninvolved.

The report we'd all worked so hard to fabricate had been bundled and transferred securely, digitally, a little more than a week before the Colonel's unscheduled arrival. It seemed odd to me that the vast bureaucracy I considered the government, and especially the military to be, could have reviewed and come to any decisions so quickly. Obviously, our biggest fear was being found out, and such a speedy assessment seemed suspect and worrisome.

Lucian, Samay, and I had played out various scenarios in lunchtime conversations. We imagined Lucian being labeled a traitor or perhaps a spy if somehow they understood he was sabotaging his own work. Maybe our worries were unfounded and even ridiculous, but the entire situation was fairly surreal, and while we didn't generally see disgraced government workers *falling* out of windows like they seemed to in Russia, we'd all seen whistleblowers and others wind up ostracized and vilified at best; jailed, lives left in ruin at worst.

During the time Lucian and his keepers were in the lab, the actual hospice nurse, a large, kind, and gentle, older black man named Evander, did arrive. He went through all his normal checks, brought more morphine, and spoke, as best he could, given her drowsy and weakened state, directly to Beverly. He was done before Lucian returned.

As Evander gathered his things and said, "I'll see you soon, beautiful," to Bev, he motioned Lily and I to follow him to the door. We walked outside onto the front landing, and Lily pulled the door nearly shut behind us.

"She's changing daily at this point," Evander said. "You've probably noticed, especially you, Dr. Roberts, but I do know that sometimes it's difficult for those closest to the patient to see the little things. Now, when something happens—Cheyne-Stokes breathing—or when the end comes, I want you to call me. Do not call 911. The DNR is in place, but sometimes paramedics can be overzealous in their desire to sustain life. I will take care of everything."

He was talking to us as if we were naïve family members instead of a seasoned oncologist and an enlightened, intelligent woman. But he was absolutely right to do so. Lily and I both stared at him with glazed looks and foggy understanding. Was that truly where we were then? How had death crept up on us all so stealthily? When had it all become this real?

We had at least a couple already, but Evander gave us three more of his business cards.

"Put them in easy-to-find places," he said.

I flushed a bit and felt my heart flutter. It was a lot to take in. We watched Evander drive away and stumbled blindly back into the house and Beverly's side. We said nothing. What was there to say?

About fifteen minutes later, Lucian and his footmen walked back into the house. The Colonel bid both Lily and me a good day, then shook Lucian's hand solemnly and left. Still reeling from Evander's assessment and directions, we braced ourselves for what Lucian had to say.

I tried to lighten the mood.

"Well, they didn't take you out in handcuffs, so that's something," I tried to joke.

He looked at us in turn and shrugged his shoulders. He looked defeated. I thought he might cry.

"I'm defunded," he said.

Lily and I looked at each other, and she hurried to his side.

"Oh baby," she said. "I'm so sorry."

I added my condolences. This was Lucian's life work, I understood, and to have it all end—even if it were an end we'd orchestrated—must have wounded him deeply. We were all losing so much here.

"It's what we wanted, though, right? What you wanted?" I ventured.

"Not what I wanted at all. Not how I wanted this to end. Just what needed to happen."

Lily hugged her husband tightly, and he, glassy-eyed, said, "They're taking the lab. Every last bit of it. It's all theirs, of course, but... 'Disassembled' Colonel Riley said. Shipped back to StratCom."

"Oh no!" Lily cried. "I mean, of course, I guess, but when?"

"A week. Maybe less. Suddenly, they're very efficient," Lucian said.

Everything about the day was spinning around me. I had that feeling of sands shifting beneath my feet again. It was what we'd wanted, been working to achieve, but I knew with the jolt of awakening to the truth that the end of Lucian's lab meant the end to any promise—if there had ever been one—of my reaching Beverly in her moment of carefree youth. And I felt the weight of a future without hope in my heart and on my chest.

My eyes welled, and I sank deep into the soft couch. My breathing seemed to quicken and then fade. I was dizzy with despair, and it all hurt.

Lily noticed my pain.

"Are you okay, Perry?" she asked. But I found it difficult to answer. I clutched my chest where the heartache grabbed and throbbed. Lucian ran to me.

"Perry...Perry! Tell me what's going on. What are you feeling?"

I found myself unable to answer but heard and saw everything around me as if I were in another bad dream.

"It's his heart! Lily, call 911! Tell them it's a heart attack!"

Lucian stayed with me. Got me on the floor with my feet elevated. Told Lily to stay with me while he ran to the lab for the defibrillator—should it become necessary. Lily tried to calm me, told me to breathe slowly.

The paramedics seemed to take hours, but in actuality, the firehouse was only a few blocks away, and they were there in minutes. Coming into the room, they saw Beverly and began to move toward her, but Lucian was just running back into the room and yelled, "It's him! It's him!"

The EMS group—three of them, two men and a woman—worked quickly. They asked all the right questions about illnesses and pre-existing conditions. Lucian explained the "one previous incident" as best he could, given the circumstances of how it had occurred. Then, we were out the door on our way to the hospital, my hospital.

Lucian yelled that he would follow, but I said—with all the strength I could muster—to stay with Beverly. I would be fine. In my head, I was sure it was just the stress of everything that had just happened so all-at-once, and I just wanted my heart healed as quickly as possible so I could be back at Beverly's side. But from my position in the back of the ambulance, I could see Lucian hadn't listened. His gray SUV was directly behind us all the way to the hospital. He entered the triage area only seconds after I'd been unloaded and rushed inside.

While my EKG had started off fairly erratic in the ambulance, it was near normal now, and I was calmer, breathing easier. Naturally, there were any number of precautionary and diagnostic tests to be done, and several hours of such followed.

Lucian was nervous. He paced the floor, clearly still wracked with guilt by the idea he and his research had somehow caused my sudden heart issues. I was far less sure *and* — as I told him over and over — even if it were true, I was the one who had asked to be a part of the research, and I fully understood the risks. I was the one, too, I also told him, whose life had been changed, who had, in effect, been cured by the miracle he was able to conjure out of wires and music and the smell of jasmine and coffee.

After several hours, a young, thin, blond, and serious-looking cardiologist named Dr. Garrity came to speak to me — to us. He was quite sure, he said, that what we were looking at was one of the conditions that generally fall under the DHD banner.

"Congenital? Me? I've never had anything come up in an exam," I told him.

"You'd be surprised how many people don't know they have a congenital heart defect until they have some kind of episode, such as the one you experienced today."

"Well, that should put your mind at ease, Lucian," I managed to laugh a bit, and the doctor raised an eyebrow. "He's just always trying to get me to exercise more," I lied.

"Hmm," Dr. Garrity wondered, "and do you tire easily when you exercise?"

"Oh, I do my best not to exercise at all," I said truthfully. "Walking these hospital halls and walking to the ballpark a few times a week from April to October is about the only exercise I take on."

There were other questions about shortness of breath, leg cramps, other arrhythmias, etcetera, and I answered them all patiently, although I was more than anxious to be out of there and back in Berkeley. I was a horrible patient, I knew, but I also knew I could worry about my own health…later.

Dr. Garrity suspected an atrial septal defect, meaning I'd had this problem — a poorly developed septum, which is the wall that separates the two upper chambers of the heart — since birth.

"A hole in my heart. I should have known," I joked. What did you do with news like this, except joke?

"We all should have known," Lucian agreed in all seriousness.

"Well, I'm sure you understand you'll need surgery as soon as possible. You've had a near miss today. You don't want another worse — or perhaps fatal — attack," the good Dr. informed me.

"I do understand, of course," I said. "But surgery will have to wait for a while."

"Wait? I'd highly advise against that."

"I know. I understand…"

"Perry," Lucian interjected. "This could be life-threatening. You need to do this now. Lily and I can take care of Beverly."

"You really should listen to your friend, Dr. Roberts. There's no reason to put your life at risk like this."

"I'm sorry Dr. Garrity. And I'm sorry Lucian. But there's not a chance in hell I'm going to have surgery right now. There will be time for surgery after Bev…well, there will be time for surgery within the next few weeks. But not today and not tomorrow, and God willing, not next week either."

"Well, I can't make you have this surgery or tell you when to have it, but again, I highly recommend you let me admit you, and we can take care of this as soon as possible. Beyond that, at least let me schedule something for you in a few weeks. Or next month?"

"Send me a couple of dates next month," I finally acquiesced. "I'll take a look and see what my schedule will allow."

This was agreeable — if not preferable — for everyone, and so it was set, and I was more than ready to be released.

"I'll have the nurse come in with instructions for your release," Dr. Garrity said. He stood to leave but turned in the doorway to add, "But, Dr. Roberts, you do understand your leaving is against my recommendations. Also, you must, absolutely must, take it easy — no strenuous exercise and avoid stressful situations as much as possible."

"I understand, and I definitely will," I told him with a straight and serious face.

After he left, Lucian looked at me and shook his head. "Perry, you should have the surgery now. You shouldn't take a chance like this! Anything could happen."

"This has been a year of nothing *but* anything-could-happens, Lucian. But there's been a lot of good, right? You have to trust me. You have to trust in the possibility of good things happening."

CHAPTER TWENTY-THREE

Beverly was awake and worried by the time I got home. It pained me to know I'd added to the burden she was already carrying, the heavy weight of dying. Of course, she also wanted me to have surgery immediately. My life was more important, she said, because I had a future to look forward to.

I didn't say anything. Bebe didn't need to know my grim and exhausting thoughts about what anything beyond that very moment looked like to me. In truth, I saw nothing beyond life with Beverly. I felt she'd flung open heavy and dark draperies that had been drawn closed most of my adult life. How was I to now live without sunlight?

We talked for a very long time about me, about us, about just about everything but her. She was busy bringing her own story to a close, yet worried only about those who were left to go on living their own.

"Perry," she whispered with her eyes closed. She was just resting them she told me. We were in the living room still — it was too much for Bev to get to and from bed these days, and Evander had scheduled a hospital bed to be delivered the next day. The couch on which she now lay would be pushed into the corner, and the new bed, the final bed, would take its place. There was no real reason to speak so softly. Lucian and Lily were upstairs, presumably asleep by now. But Beverly wanted her secrets to remain thus, or maybe it was just too much effort to make her voice heard.

"I want you to do something for me tomorrow if you would," she continued.

"Of course, anything."

"Call Ellison Peters. Ask him to come see me. But make it a time you can be here as well. And make sure it's soon, obviously."

She laughed at that, not in a feel-sorry-for-me or even ironic way. But because she just thought it was…funny.

"Will you do that for me?"

"You know I will. Everything okay?"

Ellison Peters was Bev's attorney. Her main personal attorney, that is. She had many on the payroll, but Ellison had drawn up her will and seemed to be the central lawyer to whom all the other JDs reported or at least coordinated.

"Perry," she whispered again conspiratorially. "I hear everything you know."

That laugh again.

"You might think I'm asleep, but it's just a little trick cancer has afforded me."

She smiled that Beverly smile and giggled again. I smiled too. And you know those moments? Those two smiles moments? That was what I couldn't imagine living without. I knew a smile wouldn't be worth having if Bev weren't there to share it.

"I know what's going on with Lucian," she said after a moment. "I heard him talking about being defunded today, and I know about the little conspiracy you've all been involved with."

"Oh, Bev, we didn't mean for you to worry about any of it. I'm sorry."

"Don't be sorry!" she said with sudden force. "Here I am, the one person who can do something about the situation, and you've excluded me. You've set me aside here on this couch as if I've already become a memory. I'm not a memory yet, Perry. I'm still here. I'm still very much engaged in living. That's my job, Perry. That's your job. That's all our jobs! Be engaged, Perry. That's all life asks."

I was ashamed now. How devious was my ego to talk me into shrinking from living—stepping away from Beverly while she was still here and calling me to acknowledge her being?

"I'm so sorry. Really. My God, I'm so, so sorry."

"Sorry only matters when you don't repeat the mistake," she said. It was something her father used to say to her often, and she'd carried it with her throughout her life as a kind of mantra.

"Yes," I said. "You're right. You're always right."

"Not always, but often." She chuckled again. "Perry, I'm going to talk to Ellison about funding Lucian's research. I see it within the walls of the medical center but autonomous from it. Do you think that would work?"

"I'm sure it could. I'm sure we could make it work."

"See now? That makes me happy to hear….we. With luck, I'll have time to speak with, or have Ellison or…someone, speak with the people I turn to at UCSF. They may be on board as well. It will be a little complicated, but we can get the ball rolling before I'm… not rolling balls anymore." And we both smiled again.

The scheme would require other adjustments to her will, but she'd been thinking about many of them already. I saw this wish, this promise, as indicative of the life Bev had created. Hers was a legacy that would be left to grow in many spaces where she had once stood. And who could even begin to know how these many plants would flourish in the future?

The plan for the "Bowen-Phanes Memory Research Lab" was not to be revealed to anyone until after Bev's passing. She was adamant about that. I was sworn to secrecy. She envisioned it as a grand and joyous surprise for both Lucian and Lily and felt it the least she could do for these two people she loved so dearly. Lily was to inherit stock and other things — but those were also details to which only Ellison was privy. It made Bev happy — as it always did — to know she had the ability to affect the lives of others in positive ways.

"What else is money for?" She'd asked me on many, many occasions.

I didn't know.

I contacted Ellison Peters the next morning. First thing. I called him from Beverly's phone, so he was quick to answer and happy to come see her that very day, that very morning. Such was the power of Beverly Bowen's call.

Ellison happened to arrive just before the hospital bed was delivered, and I could see his look change when the workers brought it through the front door. Beverly, still beautiful and sophisticated in her flowered dressing gown and silk head scarf, perhaps seemed to him only lounging with the weariness of ongoing illness, but the bed — a hospital bed in the living room — looked like imminence. It spoke of endings without possibility.

The bed's arrival did, in fact, help the situation. Ellison and I moved Bev to the kitchen table, only a few feet away, while the living room was rearranged, and Lily found sheets and blankets for the bed.

It wasn't preferable or comfortable for Bev to be sitting in a wooden chair at the dinner table, but it was briefly possible and private. She explained in as few words as possible what she wanted and had me speak to Ellison when her voice grew weary.

"Perry is my witness, you see, Ellison?" she asked. "I don't expect anyone to challenge my wishes. Certainly you can see I'm of sound mind, yes? But it's always good to have a witness just in case. Oh, and there's also this,"

She drew her phone out of her pocket and held it up for us to see she was recording the conversation. Trust Bev! She knew the business, and she knew, as any good ballplayer would, how to cover her bases.

Ellison laughed. He was not offended in any way. I felt him to be kind and honest—as Beverly obviously did as well—and I'd always found his relationship with her to be one of mutual respect coupled with a great deal of fondness. He was a good friend, which is what Bev deserved.

And so, with Ellison gone and the hospital bed delivered, we began a ritual of waiting—and not minding the wait. Friends and colleagues—Ruben among them—had been handling my patients for weeks and now took over full-time. There was never a worry in my mind about losing my job or credibility as a caring physician. None of it mattered. There was only Bev.

Have you, I wonder my friends, ever sat this deathbed vigil? Surely many of you have and if so, I can tell you nothing more than you already know—already have felt and experienced. But for those lucky enough—or perhaps unlucky enough—to have the great misery and great honor of standing watch the last few days and hours and minutes of a loved one's life, you understand how it is possible to both wish an end to their suffering while simultaneously willing them to hold on, live longer in whatever state they must because the thought of having them released from your physical presence—even if it means release from pain for them—is simply too much to bear.

Thus, I sat with Beverly day and night, attending to her few needs, even the most delicate, which meant to me a sweet intimacy with which she entrusted only Lily and me, and talking, reading aloud, playing music, and watching her draw shallow breaths — which whispered to me "I'm still here" — while she slept.

There was an old, upright piano that sat in the far corner of the living room, next to the stairs that led up to the main bedroom and Lily's craft room. Lily said it had come with her grandmother's house. (Too big to move out through any doorway; it had presumably been brought in before the home was finished being built and had remained like an old, welcome friend.) At some point, Lily had painted it yellow and decorated it with hand-drawn flowers. It was like Lily herself, bright and sunny, a study in nature and music.

Occasionally, Lily played the keys that she kept polished and in tune. Her playing was lovely and accomplished — again, like Lily. As the long days wore on, I came to appreciate this best friend of Beverly's — Bebe's — more and more. They were much alike, I could now see.

Each possessed an intelligence that often manifested itself as great wisdom. They spoke in short sentences that might have seemed abrupt if not so perfectly on point and frequently, even prescient. Lily maneuvered through life with a litheness that I imagined Bev possessed when she was healthy. I'd never known her as such, but even ill and with a broken arm, Bev had always moved and spoken with grace and spirit.

I thought that Beverly might have been drawn to Lily for all these same-nesses but also for the ways in which Lily's life had allowed her to express them differently. The artistic soul that dwelt within Lily had found its way out into the world and blossomed in the sunlight of belief and encouragement. People loved Lily for Lily's sake — as people embrace art and beauty on the purity of their own account.

The artistic rendering of Bev had been cut short in favor of the necessities bound up in her love for her father. They couldn't help but shine through and rise from her every move, and yet, they had never been allowed full daylight and so lay stunted and wanting far within all that moved through the world without.

Looking at Beverly now, most often asleep, sometimes unresponsive, and less and less able to communicate at all except to register pain, I longed on her behalf for the life she might have known. The life she had created was amazing and important and powerful and good, but what of the butterfly that emerges from a cocoon only to find no room to fully spread its wings?

In some ways, I thought this end — this godawful, lingering end — would release her from a box that had kept her cramped and constrained for so long. At least, I hoped. But in other ways, I so loved the woman I knew — all of her — that I would not have changed one thing about her or her life even if I could.

Except, of course, for the cancer and the damned cigarettes that had brought her to this. In college, Victoire and I had a friend named Donovan. Donovan was a smoker, and I found it incredible that anyone considering the medical profession could even think of smoking. It helped with stress, he said, and Vic had told me, "Hey, if that's the worst of his habits, I'll take it."

But now I knew why no one should ever dismiss a smoking or tobacco habit as an "I'll take it." It wasn't a personal or petty, small, bad habit. If I knew in college what I knew then, watching Bev fight to remain here, with us, with me, day after day, I would have raged at Donovan, taken his cigarettes, stomped on them, flushed them, whatever it took.

I would have looked him in the eye, taken hold of his shoulders, and said, "Don't ever make the people you love watch you die a slow, agonizing death."

The Tuesday before the Friday that was *the* day, Lucian got word the disassembling of his lab was imminent. They would be here the following Monday or perhaps over the weekend, if not sooner. Vague as ever, the message left Lucian feeling almost physically ill. Although he had saved everything he could—notes, recordings, video—in a very real sense, Lucian was about to watch his life's work taken apart and taken away.

We were all caught up in the overwhelming saga of Beverly's journey, but the government news made Lucian visibly more anxious. He began pacing the floor, doing a million little things around that house that had gone undone for years, rattling around the kitchen, threatening to deluge us with experimental meals and baked goods until Lily would send him out to walk or go with him herself to ease and guide his unwinding.

Victoire and Michael, with baby Dominique in tow, came to visit that Wednesday. I thought it was very good of them, and while Bev didn't really know—though I wanted to believe she could hear the baby cooing and eventually crying (How she loved babies!)—I still felt it meant a lot to her.

Before leaving, Victoire pulled me aside while Michael held the baby and chatted with Lily and Lucian.

"Perry," she said with urgency; the baby could need her at any second. "Samay told me about your heart."

"So much for HIPPA," I joked.

"It's no laughing matter, Perry. Look, I know you're…involved… here, but you've got to promise me you'll get the surgery as soon as… as soon as possible."

"I will. Of course, I will. And it's not a problem, I promise you."

"Not a problem? Samay said this was the second incident in only a few months!"

"He did? What else did he say?"

"Nothing specific. Just that you'd been under a great deal of stress. That you're not eating and you're not taking care of yourself and that he's worried. And I'm worried, Perry. I'm worried too."

And I could see it was true. I'm not sure why I ever thought feelings end with goodbyes. I loved Victoire then just as much as when we'd been together, and I saw now that she felt the same about me. We had decided to send our futures in different directions, but the relationship we built, the love we felt, remained the same. Our paths had only veered instead of merged.

I felt a great well of love and appreciation for Victoire rise within me. I hugged her tightly.

"Thank you for everything, Vic," I said in her ear. "You changed my life, you know that?"

When I let her go, she looked at me with eyes that threatened to spill tears.

"Perry. Take care of yourself. Michael's a basketball-only kind of guy. Who else is going to take Dominique to Giants games?"

"I'll do my best," I said.

"No, Perry. Do better than that. This isn't something to play with. This could kill you. I mean, in an instant. Please. Stay around. I need you."

We hugged again, and I told her something I should have told her so many times when I just…didn't. "I love you Victoire Royer Hines. I absolutely love you."

"I love you too, Gaylord Perry Roberts. And don't you ever forget that, okay?"

And I promised her I wouldn't.

CHAPTER TWENTY-FOUR

After Wednesday, Bev had even fewer lucid moments. Her breathing was steady, if shallow, and we all hovered around her, waiting for the slightest hint that she felt uncomfortable. Naturally, I was careful to ensure she wasn't overmedicated. But there was no need for her to be in pain either.

I watched carefully for the dreaded Cheyne-Stokes breathing—the death rattle—to begin. I'd seen it so many times, with my mother, of course, and many others. It was often frightening for families to keep their death vigils, and I understood why. In these end-of-life moments, our normal autonomic systems begin to fail, and inhaling seems to become something of an afterthought. The terminally ill, imminently expiring, sink into depths of breathlessness only to suddenly buoy up and gulp one more life-sustaining drink of air. But then they flounder once again with small, barely audible wisps that seemed only a faint memory of what breathing should be.

I could not know what this wavering between trying to live and settling into death was like for the patient, but I'd seen what those long moments—often only a few minutes, but at times, hours on end—did to those watching and saying goodbye with each exhale, yet clinging to every gasp...until that very last. Finally, the chest rose no more, and there was release—of the soul, I imagined, but also of tears, grief, and the anguish of no more goodbyes.

Very often, I also knew my dying patients would have a moment of complete lucidity even after hours of languishing in a near coma-like state. Their words sometimes spoke of people, long gone, who had come to take them home. This was quite a common occurrence, actually. At other times, the dying comforted the living, telling them not to cry or fear or hesitate to move forward. I'd never witnessed any patient panicking or afraid—not at the very end. That came more often at diagnosis or during treatment. But at the end, the very end, peace came like an old friend, a reminder that pain-free times of no worry and tangible joy did exist. I think this peace may have also whispered a promise of eternity.

By Friday—*that* Friday—the StratCom team still hadn't shown up, and because Beverly was so close to slipping away, we had hoped for a private weekend with no interruptions, save it be from death itself.

Midmorning, however, Samay messaged to ask if he and Lien could stop by later in the day. Lien had called me more than once and been tender and kind in our conversations. Samay had been much the same, albeit more awkwardly. I would be very happy to see them, I said. And it was true. I was happy to have their company.

Lily had been playing piano for Bev occasionally and it set a lovely tone. I appreciated her skill and choice of music, which always seemed right, even though I often didn't know the tune she played.

That day, she instead decided to play some of Beverly's vinyl collection. Lily said she would play the records because she couldn't play the piano.

"Not today. Just...not today," she told me.

Over the weeks and little by little, we'd seemed to have brought most of Beverly's LPs to the house. She'd ask us to play one song or another or one full album or series of albums, and off we'd go to "the big house," as we jokingly called it, to retrieve another memory for Bev.

That day, we began with gentle music, some classical: Debussy and Bach. Later, we played her favorites from her favorite era, The Carpenters and Simon and Garfunkel. Arlo Guthrie sang to Bev, "Go to sleep, you weary hobo," and we all hid our glistening eyes from each other.

And then Lily said, "I know you love this one, Bebe." And it was John Denver singing, "Today while the blossoms still cling to the vine…"

And she kept clinging and I willed her to never stop.

Samay and Lien showed up midafternoon and were visibly shaken by Bev's condition. The last time they'd seen her, she was propped up and talking. We'd laughed about, well, me mostly, and I had plenty of foibles and missteps to make for many stories and lots of joke-making. Funny how nothing seems at your expense when it's making someone you love let go and just…laugh.

That Friday—*the* Friday—was much different. Bev's eyes were closed—they hadn't really been open since Wednesday. She was impossibly thin, and her body slightly curved, as if trying to move into the fetal position, only to have given up midway at the impossibility of it.

Still, these two friends, a true couple now, rallied and greeted us—all of us—with warmth.

"How are you holding up?" Lien wanted to know.

"I'm okay. Hanging in there," I said. It was an answer I had repeated many times over the past several weeks and days."

"But how are you feeling, Perry? Weakness? Shortness of breath? Pain?" Samay queried me more closely.

"I'm fine, Samay. I'm staying as calm as I possibly can."

"We're invoking peace," Lily added. "Trying to…for all our sakes."

And then, suddenly, and very unexpectedly, Beverly opened her eyes. She didn't move her head, but her eyes surveyed the room.

"The gang's all here," she half-whispered with the slightest of smiles.

"We're all here for you, Bebe," Lily said.

I took her frail hand.

"Right here with you, Bev," I said.

"Of course, Perry. I knew you would be…" Her voice trailed off, and her eyes began to close, but just before they did, she added, "You'll find me, Perry, won't you?"

"Yes, Beverly, my love. Yes, of course I'll find you. Someday I'll find you…" and now it was my voice that choked and then keened. I cried openly and ferociously, and when I was finally able to gather myself, I understood everyone else was crying too. Of course, we were. Had we not been sharing this moment of grief, it would have been too much for any one of us to bear.

And then I noticed.

A gasp and a long, slow exhale. A moment of silence, then a shallow breath.

It had started.

My mind raced. All these days of waiting and understanding the process and now that it was actually happening, I couldn't comprehend an ending. I became frantic, manic. I breathed deeply, willing Bev to do the same, and she tried. By God, she tried.

"Lucian," I said with strength and determination. "We need to… we have to get Bev to the lab right now."

"What? What are you talking about, Perry? Are you insane?"

"No, not insane! I'm perfectly rational, but this can't be the end! This can't be the end, Lucian!"

I was sputtering and crying but also serious and very, very determined.

"You heard her! She asked me to find her!"

"Perry, she meant one day. You know that day we all meet again…" Lily tried gently to reassure me.

"No! It's now! It has to be now." I was talking through gritted teeth now. Trying to sound rational and knowing time was slipping away. "Please, my God, please, Lucian. At least try! Let us try! Just one shot, one chance to see her healthy and happy and young and…alive! Please, Lucian, if you care anything for Beverly or for me, please try!"

Lucian looked at Samay, then Lily and Lien. No one nodded approval. How could they? It was an irrational and dangerous thing to do, but…they knew it might work. They knew it might help me move on. They'd seen it work for me before. And yet…

"It's not safe for *you*, Perry. Your heart! What if something happened? How could I live with myself?"

"You could live with yourself because you'd know—you'd absolutely know that this is what I wanted. That I begged you for this chance! That one more real minute with Bev alive and happy was worth more to me than a million without her. Please—I absolve you of any blame or guilt—all of you!" I stood and looked each one in the eye. "Now, please, can we hurry? Please!"

And we did. Beverly weighed no more than a thought, and we easily carried her—blankets, pillows, and all—to the lab. Shaking his head all the while, Lucian quickly affixed the connected skullcaps to our heads. He fired everything up and asked himself and Samay, "What next?"

He was rushing, and so caught up in the irrationality of the moment, he'd lost his normal sense of systematic maneuvering and methodical planning.

"Bev needs nothing, obviously," he said.

We all stopped and looked at her as she gasped for another short breath. We were silent, waiting to see if there would be another or if we were too late. But she breathed again. She breathed again!

"This is insanity," Lucian said mostly to himself.

"Something for me," I said. "Something to help me relax. No pheno obviously, but something."

Samay knew where things were and readied an injection of Demerol.

"I'm not giving you all of this," he said as he gave me the injection.

"I don't even know how to find a memory in Bev. Am I supposed to just stimulate blindly? That's ridiculous! Like finding a needle in a haystack!" Lucian was nearly frantic now, and even as I relaxed, I felt time slipping away and feared my chance, my one chance, was nearly gone.

But I suddenly remembered something and reached for my phone.

"Here," I said, scrolling through songs, "play this. Hold it close to her ear."

Lily took my phone from me and stood by Bev, holding the phone nearly against her ear. In a moment, the calliope began to turn, and it oom-pahed into the room with a gaiety that flew in our faces and defied the whole bizarre scene. I was truly drowsy now, but I could hear Lucian say, "My God. It's working! I've got it! I've got the memory! Relax, Perry. Listen to the music…"

And I did. I let it fill me and surround me until suddenly. It stopped. It was gone.

"It's dead," Lily said.

But she was talking about my phone. Good God, how had I forgotten to charge it? Of course, my days had been filled with Beverly, Beverly, Beverly…but in all my thoughts of helping her, I had failed to do the simplest of things, and now, in this hour—this ultimate hour of saving her, being with her—I had failed! I had failed Beverly, and I had failed myself.

I cannot begin to explain the pain of realizing I'd botched such a simple task and knowing I'd ruined it all. My mind was filled with a thousand thoughts at once in the way that happens when your life faces a crisis—a beginning or an end. Why now? What did this mean? Was this the end then? And even as I began to give up, my mind fought to find a solution. How do I fix this? I wanted to explain the song and how to find it again on one of their own phones, but I was also fighting the effects of the Demerol, and the words I was thinking were already slipping away. They seemed to spill out of my head and dissipate into a mist that wouldn't form words.

I heard Lucian, dear Lucian, yell for all of them to murmur as if a crowd. It was a ridiculous request. Silly, really, but Lucian knew the scene I was trying to recreate. We'd talked about it when I first ventured this idea with him. It was all he could think to do, and I loved him for it. I didn't believe it would work, and I doubt anyone else did either, but they complied, and I felt a tear slip from my closed eye and spill down the side of my face. I felt Beverly was lost. And I was lost. We were lost.

My heart began to beat haphazardly—noncommittally, and I started to surrender to the pain, the future, the sedation, all of it.

Just then, from Beverly's side came a clear voice, a wholesome sound. I might have thought it an angel had I not recognized Lily's pure vibrato.

"Today, while the blossoms still cling to the vine," she sang, "I'll taste your strawberries. I'll drink your sweet wine. A million tomorrows shall all pass away ere I forget…"

And with my eyes closed to Lucian and Lily and Samay and Lien, all that was Gaylord Perry Roberts began to fade…

But then, in a moment, I blinked and squinted. It was the sun. So bright on this early morning and so alive with the crowd and the carousel and the costumes and a recent college grad dressed in a bright orange sailor top and knickers velcroed at the knee and with her long blond hair pulled into a ponytail. I stared in recognition and in love…as always. She felt my look and turned to face me, and in some way, we knew…again. And she smiled.

And somewhere in the air above my head, I thought I heard Lucian yelling something like, "His heart! We're losing him!"

Then, the steady beep of a flat line that somehow merged with a singular note from the carousel song, which grew louder with voices now, "See the carousel, turning round and around there. It's a fantasy. Take a ride, and you'll see."

And I saw. Everything became denser and more real; the smells, the sounds, the feel, and more tangible than anything: Beverly.

My heart beat strong and steady, and I stayed.

EPILOGUE

My focus has been here now for nearly fifty years. Focus. You see, it's exactly as Lily hypothesized. I am where my focus is. I was helped here, as you now well know, by all of them — my friends, our friends — though Beverly never knew them in this timeline.

And you see, that is what I believe happened. A sort of time travel, yes, but along with it, a hop, a skip over to another path, a parallel life, if you will. My personal belief is that, in some way, all of our timelines are connected, and someday, when our focus is back in the purely nonphysical realm, I — we — will know them all. These truths I expect to know soon, for as I mentioned at the beginning of my story, I am dying…again.

But, I am approaching eighty years old, which is a long time to live and relive. Throughout all these many decades, Beverly has been by my side. As she still is today. Healthy, you ask? Why of course she is. She never took up smoking. I dissuaded her from ever trying, and there was no need anyway.

Let me tell you that from that first day, the first day in the amusement park, we were inseparable. This is our truth, and I believe it plays out on every one of the timelines we share and always will. I had nothing, of course, when I reappeared in Beverly's life, but I was smart and industrious, and…luckily, thankfully, it was a much different time. New lives could be created from obituaries found in library archives, and birth certificates obtained for a few dollars from the local office of vital records. Thus, I was reborn.

I never even attempted to redo medical school and become a doctor again—although my knowledge was quite useful on a number of occasions, including persuading Beverly's father to have his heart checked thoroughly and helping him convalesce after his quadruple bypass during my first few weeks here. My M.D. was the byproduct of another timeline, one that seemed to demand my study and degree as a kind of pardon from the crime of having a mother ill with cancer.

As for Beverly, there was no need for her to take over the company in her youth, and when it was eventually handed to her—well, us—some twenty years later, we decided to leave it in the hands of those who had mostly been running it anyway while we managed the philanthropic arm of the organization. But even after we began running The Bowen Charitable Trust, we had time for the things we loved—the promises we had made to each other and family.

You have so many questions running through your head. Is everything the same here as it was on my Perry Roberts timeline? The answer is yes. And no. Just as I am able to follow different roads here, so are others. You can imagine I was eager to find my mother—perhaps meet another me like in some episode of The Twilight Zone. But no. Another me didn't exist here, and while I didn't find my mother in the Bay Area years after my arrival, as the internet took hold here (as in my ex-life), I was able to search for and find her under her maiden name with a new name added that was not Roberts. She, too, had chosen differently in this iteration of her existence, and I was happy for her to have had a longer and perhaps happier life. At least, I hoped that was the case.

There is more to say about others, but as I became immersed in this life, comparing it with my old life became less and less important. Beverly and I spent our days together, and that was all that mattered.

You wonder now if I ever told her. But if you have read my entire story, how can you suppose I could ever keep a secret from my Bebe? I didn't tell her that first day and, in fact, not for months — after I'd found my new identity, secured a job, and was able to pay for my stay on Bev's couch. Yes, she had allowed me in that first night. I had thought to move slowly. The last thing I wanted was to push her away. Where would I be then?

But although everything was different, our meeting played out much the same as it had when I first diagnosed a sick and injured Beverly, and we could never part again. Bev wanted to know my name that first night, of course, and I — having yet to secure a new identity — told her the only thing I could think of on the spot: Sam.

Have you ever had to think of something quickly, urgently, and in that split second between question asked and question answered, had a whole confluence of possibilities and ideas run through your head in an instant? So it was with me that sunny March morning. Asked my name and who I was, the truth sprang into my head. Gaylord Perry Roberts. But no, obviously, that wouldn't do, not here, where I had to find a new life and, with it, a new name. But in those same few seconds, I thought of the real Gaylord Perry's nickname: the Ancient Mariner. It reminded me of the poem Professor Adams had assigned us in my college freshman English class, *The Rime of the Ancient Mariner.* It was a long and difficult journey to decipher the tale of an adventure by sea to another land. Much of it was lost on the eighteen-year-old me, but at that moment, I felt a sudden kinship to it. And while there was no Sam in the story, well, surely you know the author.

Days later, searching old newspapers for a possible new identity, I came across a likely candidate, Geoffrey Samuel Mortenson, and it fit well enough. You may have seen my work as GS Mortenson; easier to sign a painting as such. It was funny because even when Beverly's sweet lips first formed the name "Sam," she seemed to mistrust it. Told me, in fact, that it didn't suit me. All these years later, I'm still tailoring, trying to get a decent fit.

We naturally progressed as a couple, and when it shortly became undeniable Beverly Bowen would be willing to become Beverly Bowen Mortenson, I took her to the beach. Yes, Ocean Beach. Our important talks seemed always to belong there. And I confessed. There was the risk she might think me insane. But the story I told her is the same one I have told you here and do you doubt my sanity? Then imagine how much easier it was for Beverly, who knew me so well, who I felt as an extension of my own self or perhaps the force that made me my own self, to consider the tale.

"And did I die? Did we both die, do you suppose?" This Beverly asked as I finished my story, our story.

"In that timeline, that life, I suppose we did."

"And our friends grieved for us, didn't they, Sam? Or should I call you Perry?"

"They grieved for us, I'm sure. I only hope they didn't blame themselves for my choices. My heart was bad; that was a fact, but I pushed, and I'm sure they did what they could. Hopefully, they didn't—don't—blame themselves."

"But here we are now. Again. Together. I wish I remembered or could focus even for a few minutes on that other life," she said.

"It was a wonderful but difficult life. Too much pain, I'm afraid. Especially for you. You wouldn't want to feel all that," I assured her.

"Oh, but I would, Sam. How could I not want to know more, share more with you? How could I not want to lean on you and have you lean on me in any new or different way, no matter the circumstances, no matter the cost?"

Perhaps you understand now, with every new line I write in my story, how I could have loved Beverly in two lifetimes, and who knows? Maybe many more.

Certainly, our children understand how we feel. They tease us unmercifully about it, and we love every minute of it. Cecily was born in Paris when I was studying art, and Bev was working toward her Ph.D. She was finished by the time Daniel was born only three years later, and we were quite well established in our various careers—she writing and teaching; me painting and remembering—when Geoffrey Samuel, Jr. (called Sammy, sometimes pronounced reflexively by me as Samay) was born three years after that.

We are now a family of in-laws and grandchildren and even great-grandchildren, and I see pieces of Bev, pieces of me and my mother, and Daniel E. Bowen in each one of them. They are an expansion of ourselves in this timeline, and I'm awed by the miracle of it.

We have not lived our lives exclusively or even mainly in the Bay Area, although Bowen Enterprises does keep a box at Oracle Park, and we visit often, including, as tonight, for a yearly family reunion with all the Mortensons who can make it. Our family get-together always coincides with a fundraising event for pediatric cancer, and tonight, we also will announce, to some special guests, that a new laboratory is to be formed, funded by our foundation and dedicated to the pursuit of understanding memory and utilizing such knowledge to treat many kinds of emotional and even physical trauma.

There is a young doctor here in San Francisco—or actually, nearby Berkeley—named Lucian Phanes, and I believe he will discover much and accomplish many great things. He has been invited to attend with his wife, Lily, a true inspiration and preternaturally talented. Beverly has not yet met them, but she will love them, of this, I am sure. Other representatives of the hospital where the lab will reside have also been invited. Those guests, the ones who have followed similar paths in this timeline (which is to say virtually everyone), I am also looking forward to meeting…again. And though I am now an old man, failing in health, and Beverly, younger than me, but older now than when we all knew her in our previous lives, I believe there will be recognition. Some kind of recognition.

Because, you see, in the end, we are all connected, not only to all our lives and experiences but to each other. There is no one lost because, in truth, we cannot stray. We change and experiment and challenge ourselves and learn and grow within this spacious present. And it is big enough for all of us and everything we want and need to learn and do.

So, now you know my story.

And though it ends here, know that I do not. Beverly does not. Our stories evolve and change and expand as we try on new lives and parallel lives, and it's all beautiful. And it is the same for you, I promise.

ABOUT THE AUTHOR

An award-winning journalist, **Kris Middaugh** spent two-decades working in print media, first as a writer and reporter and later as an editor and publisher. She retired from journalism in 2018 and was caretaker for her mother for several years before again turning her attention to writing fulltime.

A Million Tomorrows is the third novel from Kris Middaugh. Her previous works include *Particles of Faith* and the co-authored *Kintyre Girls*, with Christina Sudairy. Kris grew up in San Jose, California and recently returned to the area to be closer to family. Contact Kris Middaugh via Rebel Publishing.

Made in United States
Cleveland, OH
06 April 2025